TWO TER...
OF...

When this amazing autobiography was first published by a small paperback house in 1961, it sold for 50¢ and its conservative print-run sold out immediately. Used book stores never seemed to carry dog-eared copies in their racks of discarded reading matter. MEMOS FROM PURGATORY seemed to have vanished; but those who had bought the book kept it, passed it on from friend to friend; and by 1969 it had become an underground cult item that caused an even smaller West Coast publisher to bring out a second edition. Today, copies of that first edition sell for over seventy dollars in antiquarian bookshops—when they can get a copy; and the second edition can't be pried away from those who own it by threats or coercion. Now, with an updated introduction by its incomparable author, MEMOS returns to print in Ace Books's definitive program of Ellison titles. Now you can find out what the hell all the excitement's been about.

BOOKS BY HARLAN ELLISON

- ■ Available in Ace Books editions.
- ● Forthcoming in Ace Books editions.

HARLAN ELLISON
MEMOS FROM PURGATORY

ACE BOOKS, NEW YORK

MEMOS FROM PURGATORY

An Ace Book / published by arrangement with
the author

PRINTING HISTORY
Ace edition / November 1983

NOTE: Brief passages from Book Two: "The Tombs" appeared in *The
Village Voice,* copyright 1960, by The Village Voice, Inc., as "Buried in the
Tombs," and are used here in greatly expanded form.

*The incidents presented in this book are true. They occurred to the author in
the manner described and in the periods of time designated. However—
cliches be damned—in some cases the names and dates have been changed
to protect not only the lost and the innocent, but occasionally—unfortu-
nately—the guilty. In Book Two: "The Tombs" the author would very much
have liked to use the real names of two culprits, but anonymity seemed the
most deserving fate, infamy being too bloody rewarding.*

ISBN: 0-441-52438-9

Ace Books are published by The Berkley Publishing Group,
200 Madison Avenue, New York, N.Y. 10016.
PRINTED IN THE UNITED STATES OF AMERICA

Letter received by the author:

May 1, 1972

Dear Mr. Ellison:

My name is Julie Sherman and I'm the daughter of Madeline and Ed Sherman. I am writing you to tell you of some bad news that has happened. On April 16, my mother died. The reason I am telling you is because you dedicated your book, MEMOS FROM PURGATORY, to my father and therefore I thought you were a friend of my mother.

I know that in matters such as "death" you should personally call the person and not say it in a letter. But since you're all the way in California, and I'm all the way in New York, it seems impossible.

Maybe some day you can write a book and dedicate it to my mother. Thank you.

Sincerely,

Julie Sherman

MEMO '83

Eight years have elapsed since the last time I wrote an update to this book. In 1954 when the events chronicled in *Book One: The Gang* occurred, I was just about twenty years old. In 1960, the experiences I chronicled as *Book Two: The Tombs* happened to an Ellison who was twenty-six, had been married and divorced, had been in the Army, and was well into the beginning of his writing career.

In 1969, when the first updated introduction was written, I was already thirty-five, had been through two more marriages and divorces (on the theory that I'd keep trying till I got it right), had moved to Los Angeles, was writing books, movies and television, and was a world removed from the punk who'd joined the Barons fifteen years earlier. By 1975, when this book was published for the third time—demonstrating a viability I could never have guessed when I sat in that basement in Evanston, Illinois in 1961 writing it—I was a forty-one-year-old man who still had one more marriage and divorce lying in wait for him, had already published a substantial body of work, and had begun to realize that I might live to a nasty old age.

It is now spring of 1983 and MEMOS FROM PURGATORY blooms once again, like the lemon and tangerine trees in my backyard here in the City of the Angels. By the time Ace Books publishes this new edition, I will be forty-nine. Next year it's half a century. Jeezus!

There were days in 1954, in Brooklyn, when I was more than damned dead certain I would not live to reach age twenty-one. (Similar days had occurred when I was age fourteen, but then, I suppose we all shared *that* go-to-hell cynicism.) But Fate and Gravity have not yet punched my ticket, and as I sit here ruminating on the tenacity with which this meager chronicle has clung to life, I am warmed not only by the sweet breezes blowing across the San Fernando Valley, but by the better than 50/50 chance that MEMOS said something right in 1961 that may provide a shot at Posterity. When you're in sight of fifty; and acne cases who think The Beatles were maybe an ancient cadre who marched on the Children's Crusade occasionally try to piss you off by calling you an old fart; and you know if you were to go down to East L.A. to try and ferret out the current status of gang life that would update the reminiscences in this book, that you'd be too slow to get out of the way of something sharp and shiny; knowing that you wrote something two and a half lifetimes earlier that still has some music in it makes the springtime seem well worth waiting for.

Hoping you're the same...

HARLAN ELLISON
9 April 83
Los Angeles

MEMO '75

What goes around . . . comes around.

What happens in this book happened to me in 1954 and 1960. The world was a certain way then. Let's call it Situation A. By the time this book was published the first time, the 1954 portion of Situation A was fast fading, almost gone. The 1960 portion still obtained; the book was done in 1961. By the time the second edition was released through a tiny West Coast publisher in a very limited edition in 1969, Situation A was long-gone and, in the introduction to that second edition (which follows this new preface), the world had become another kind of place. Situation B.

It is now six years later. 1975. My observations about street gangs in 1969 no longer hold. Not even remotely. In fact, I was dead-ass wrong. Or, as Santayana put it, "Those who cannot remember the past are condemned to repeat it." Situation B, as described in *Memo '69*, never reached fruition. It was all wishful thinking on my part. I won't go any further on that line: read *Memo '69* and you'll see the pathetic wish-fulfillment of my statements just six years ago. (Current, cynical observations can be found in my collection APPROACHING OBLIVION.)

But the point that needs to be made here, *especially*

here, is that we didn't go into a Situation C, for God's sake, we wound up back at square one, in Situation A.

Not only didn't I learn from the past, I didn't even see it come barreling back at me from the opposite direction. But *this* time, I think, I hope——I'd damned well better had——I got that truck's number when it hit me.

There's no need to write an extensive new description of street gangs in the 1970's, of violence and death, kids invading schoolyards and even schoolrooms to shoot down members of rival clubs . . . because it's all in the book as it happened in 1954.

What goes around . . . has come around.

In Chicago the black gangs Back O' The Yards are locked in constant, deadly combat. In Manhattan's Chinatown and out in San Francisco, the Oriental clubs restage the Tong Wars. In East L.A. the Chicano gangs are so tough not even the hardiest newspaper reporters can get in to report the machinations of warfare. In South Boston . . . well, to *hell* with the white assholes of South Boston.

MEMOS FROM PURGATORY has suddenly, sadly, become relevant again.

You can't *believe* how sad that makes me.

As for the second part of this book, about jail, well, things ain't much different now than they were then. Yeah, they're closing down Manhattan's Tombs, but they've still got to stick people away somewhere, and we've got the bitter aftertaste of Attica to heighten our appetite for the slam. And in state and federal joints all across this nation the white and hispanic and black gangs proliferate; and if you don't join, you walk a tightrope over doom.

I don't know where else to go with this introduction. It all seems so damnably inevitable, so helpless-making. I should have seen it, and I didn't, and I feel like a jerk. Leo Dillon, who did the cover for the first edition—a portrait of me behind bars—and who did the cover for this new edition, said just the other night that I keep fooling myself, that I keep murmuring *spero meliora,* I hope for better things, but that in my gut, in the outer layers of my skin, in my non-sentimental sections of brain, I *know* it's all the same, always the same, always going to *be* the same. Maybe Leo's right; I don't know.

All I know is that in 1963 when Hitchcock did MEMOS as the first of his hour-long tv shows, he had James Caan (in his first major Hollywood role) playing Harlan Ellison, and I wasn't hip enough to know that some day he'd be a star, having climbed to fame and glory in the role of Sonny Corleone in *The Godfather*. And if I couldn't even see that one day they'd be totemizing the slug creatures of the Mafia as charming, homeloving businessmen who only kill occasionally to protect the family business, then how the hell could I be expected to understand that the conditions of life and the pressures of desperation that made the kids and the jails what they were in the first place would come full-circle—because they've never been gone— to send the kids out in the streets again?

Listen: it's twenty-one years since I went out into the swamp to get the background that resulted in this book and three others. It's fourteen years since the book you hold came out the first time. And six since the second edition with its starry-eyed preface filled with bullshit and wish-fulfillment. Maybe in another five years, if this book has a continued life . . . and at this point it looks like *nothing* can kill it . . . short of universal brother/sisterhood, which I think is highly unlikely . . . I'll be back at this typewriter, saying something different.

Maybe I'll be smiling and reporting back that we've reached Situation C at last. Maybe we'll be back at B. And probably we'll still be mired down at Situation A.

Maybe not. But I doubt it.

Santayana was right, I now believe. What goes around . . . comes around.

Hey, why don't you all make a liar out of me again. Be nice to each other and watch the Ellison look like a *shmuck*. If that isn't impetus enough, then think about some kid lying face-down in an empty parking lot with

10

his head blown open by a $35 piece he bought off the street; and while *that* one's still burning, think about the kid who pulled the trigger, growing old and maggoty in some jail cell.

That's right, Billy Graham, it's a terrific world. Where do I go for a refund on my ticket?

HARLAN ELLISON
11 December 74
New York City

MEMO '69

Eight years ago, the book you are about to read was first published. It was released by a very small paperback house in Evanston, Illinois, with a print order of just over a hundred thousand copies. It sold for fifty cents a copy. About six months ago, I received—as a matter of course— a catalogue of rare and out-of-print volumes from an antiquarian bookshop in San Francisco. This book, in its original incarnation, was listed at fifteen dollars, with the amended notation that it was in VG condition.

When MEMOS FROM PURGATORY was published, the events of the first section—the time I spent with the gangs in Brooklyn—were already seven years past, though the events of the second section—jail time in Manhattan—were only a year gone. It all started in 1954, it saw print in 1961, and now it is 1969. Fifteen years later, and yet another edition of that book is being published. For an autobiography dealing with a subject as specialized as kid gangs and incarceration, it is extremely peculiar that a decade and a half could pass, and the book will compel interest. History's memory is notoriously short.

Yet here is the strangest part of it all:

In fifteen years of scrounging through used paperback stores, I have never *ever*, even once, in Detroit, Cleveland, Chicago, New York, Miami, Kansas City or Los Angeles . . .

ever seen a copy of this book among the cast-off remnants of a nation's spare time reading matter.

The original publisher, now defunct, assured me, some five years ago, when I wrote asking for a dozen copies, that he had none available. The warehouse to which returned copies had been sent had depleted its supply long since. So, though there were undoubtedly returns, even *they* had been sold, either to dealers who had had reorders, or to collectors who may have sensed there was something worth saving in the book . . . or, more probably, to casual readers who had heard about the book in the literary underground. It would have had to have been word-of-mouth, for as far as I know, MEMOS FROM PURGATORY (unlike the companion volume of short stories, GENTLEMAN JUNKIE & OTHER STORIES OF THE HUNG-UP GENERATION, issued by the same publisher at the same time, and now even more of a rare book than MEMOS) was never reviewed by a major publication or newspaper.

But apparently the word has passed. I heard some of the word myself. A few letters, one every year or so, from guys who had been in the slammer, telling me they dug the book, that it captured many of the thoughts and experiences they had themselves had. A passing phrase from another writer, at a workshop, casually mentioning "that jail book" I'd written. But nothing major, nothing really sensational, no brushfire of enthusiasm such as the kind that picked up Pollini's work, or James Drought's, or even Tolkien's books. Just a steady coterie of fans who saved their copies, thus making copies in VG condition worth fifteen bucks. With the exception of GENTLEMAN JUNKIE, none of my other books—books that sold far better, and had far greater circulation—commanded that kind of perennial interest. And about five years ago, I started getting letters from readers who wanted to know if *I* had copies I'd mind selling.

Now, it is 1969, fifteen years after the days I walked the garbage-scented streets of Bedford-Stuyvesant. Fifteen years after I lived in a rented room so small the mice were

13

hunchbacked. Fifteen years since I worked with a 12-inch Italian stiletto and fifteen years since I wrote my first novel, based on the experiences in this autobiography.

There are some updatings to be done, of course, which is what impels this new introduction.

The situation in the streets has changed drastically. For the most part, the juvie gangs are gone. Well, not really gone, because the reasons for their existence still exist—the poverty, the alienation, the helplessness, the hopelessness of their lives, their need to belong to something meaningful. But they've changed. The black gangs have now become militant civil rights groups, a la the Blackstone Rangers in Chicago. The organizational talents of many of the gang leaders and their war councillors has been channeled into student dissent on college campuses. And, I'm sorry if you're a right-winger and find what I'm about to say odious, it's a beautiful thing. Those kids never had anything of their own . . . except the gangs. They lacked pride in self, pride in race, pride in nation. So they banded together in the streets, to form artificial clans, little communities built on violence. But the new dawning of passion among the young in this country, in this time of intellectual and emotional upheaval, has given them something concrete and lovely to which they can belong.

They are suddenly concerned for their lives, these damned and forgotten children of the streets. They are—miracle!—concerned for their world. They see what a hideous, fucked-up garbage dump their elders have made of this nice green ball of sod whirling through the universe, and they may not know they are in the best traditions of Thoreau and the American Revolution, but they have ceased their internecine warfare and have turned all that hostility and guerrilla expertise against the Establishment.

Well, I say *great*.

Instead of being a force for destruction in our big cities, the kids have now become a core of fighters to liberate the black man, to hand back some of the responsibility of their futures to the young people who must live those lives, to

14

bludgeon to death once and for all the outmoded and guilt-drenched moralities that have kept this nation so schizoid for so long. The job was foisted off on them—all they really wanted to do was hang around the stoops and get in a few bops from time to time. But even without truly understanding what a force for change and good they are, the very gangs of which I speak in this book, gangs that fifteen years ago were able to terrorize entire neighborhoods, these same gangs have become the front ranks of a youth movement that will certainly revolutionize and uplift not only *this* country, but the world.

That the rebel always looks like an outlaw when he first begins his march toward the light, is a reality even history cannot dim or forget. So though the gang kids may look like the ragtag tatter of an alien horde, they are, in fact, the one genuine hope for our times.

The changes in me during the past fifteen years cannot compare in terms of radicalism with the way in which these kids have changed themselves.

So this book is outdated. No doubt about it. But so are books about the French Revolution . . . so are books about Castro's wresting Cuba from a dictator . . . so are books about Mexico's struggle for freedom . . .

What was a book of instant immediacy, fifteen years ago, has become a chronicle of a period. In a sense, a lot of history. Yet I am still reminded of those letters from people who have said this book gave something special to them, in a special way, and speaks to the human condition in general, not just to juvenile delinquency or the prison system in particular.

And for that reason, for those seemingly permanent joys and truths herein contained, this book has retained its hold on life. Till now, another edition emerges.

Many of you may have seen a vastly changed and fictionalized version of this book on Alfred Hitchcock's television series. It was purchased by the Hitchcock organization in 1962, and appeared over NBC in 1963. The title was the same, but it was hardly consistent with the truth of what really happened. I mention that show, and the subject of truth, because in the most important ways that is what this book is about.

And since I'm dealing here with truth, I must answer for the first time in print the question of those who've read this volume, who ask me, "Did everything in that book really happen?"

The answer is a simple yes. Precisely as reported. There is, however, one deviation from chronological and specific fact. In section two, "The Tombs," chapter thirteen, I wrote that I met Pooch, one of the gang kids I'd known, while in jail. That is a lie. The boy whom I refer to as Pooch was a nameless kid whom I'd never met before we wound up in the same slammer. When I handed in the manuscript of this book to its original publisher, he had only one quarrel with the way it was written. He felt there might not be enough linkage between the two sections, and he asked if I could change the kid in the slammer to one of the kids from the gang, thereby tying the two sections together. After considerable thought, I agreed. They had been so much alike, merely to give that nameless kid a name (which was a dreamed-up name to begin with), seemed to me to be a harmless untruth. So I did it. No one ever seemed to notice, or find fault with the coincidence. But through the years that one untruth has rankled me.

Now that I've taken this space to set it straight, I can answer with clear conscience, "Yes, everything in this book was real, was true, happened just this way. And the truths that emerge from it are still true."

Because truth never changes.

Not really.

The forces that warped and shaped the lives of which I speak in this book, still maintain. They are still at work. They still cripple lives, communities, an entire nation.

What comes down in this book is a total picture. A tapestry, if you will, of degradation and the killing pressures that turn people to shit. If, after fifteen years, you still find moments while reading in which your stainless steel

16

hearts soften a bit, then I have done my job well, and this part of my life that I spent compiling sights and smells and sounds, to weave into the tapestry, will not end as merely another dog-eared remnant of someone's leisure-time reading.

This book is very dear to me, very personal and important to me. I hope it has value for you.

For truly, a writer is only what he writes.

HARLAN ELLISON
Los Angeles, 1969

A MESSAGE FROM THE SPONSOR:

There is a jazz humorist named Ed Sherman who writes a column called "Out Of My Head" for Down Beat, the music bi-weekly. He also cut a record on Riverside with some of his routines. Unwittingly, George Crater (that's Sherman's pseudonym) gave me the point of this book. He invented the "wind-up doll." Like the Ornette Coleman wind-up doll that comes complete with a little plastic sax, that you wind up and set down on the table—and it forgets the chords. Or the Horace Silver doll that you wind up and set down on the table and it sweats. Or, to extrapolate, the Nikita wind-up doll that you wind, set down on the table—and it takes off its shoe; or the Eichmann doll that comes complete with a letter of authorization from its higher-ups, that when you wind up and set down on the table—cops out. You see, the point of this book is that I've got this Common Man wind-up doll . . .

PROLOGUE

There are two kinds of people with whom this book is chiefly concerned. The lost and the guilty.

Appearance is not always reality, and the ones who may on the surface appear to be the guilty, too often are merely the lost ones, the damned ones, the children of the gutters, and the faceless faces seen below the Earth in a section of the New York metropolitan jail system known as "The Tombs."

This book is a chronicle of two periods in my life spent gathering material. Once intentionally, once by the accidental design of someone else (Fate?); but both in common by the mark of memory they have made on me.

I am not a crusader. I am not a bushy-bearded fanatic screaming for reform. I am a writer. My life is the sum total of the words I have set down on paper, and their truth to me, and to those who read them.

In this book my truth concerns the kids we call juvenile delinquents, and the truth I saw while in the Tombs for twenty-four hours in 1960. The first led to the second.

These pages will relay the signs, sounds, emotions and textures of what I saw. But the jail sequence was only the smallest part of it. For the background was a ten-week sojourn among the kid gangs of Red Hook, Brooklyn, the deadliest section of a slum area breeding more potential

19

criminals per day than John Edgar Hoover could stamp out in a decade.

But before you can understand the truth as I saw it in the gang, or in the Tombs, you must understand me.

My name is Harlan Ellison. At this writing I'm twenty-seven years old. When I was eighteen I decided I wanted to be a writer. I attended Ohio State University, and after discovering writing is a thing of the genes, not the schoolrooms, I left college to attempt a professional career behind the typewriter. I hit New York City in 1954 and worked at odd jobs until I had sold enough stories to quit and free-lance full time. At one point, I decided what the subject of my first novel would be. That point came on the corner of 45th and Broadway in New York City.

It came when I saw a gang of young boys, their shoulders thrown back, their chests covered by black leather, their feet bound up in heavy Army boots—just right for stomping. Across their backs they had blazoned in script, BLOODED ROYALS. They were the first members of an organized kid gang I had ever seen, and there was something terrible and uncompromising in them.

Novelists who prate about the eyes as giveaways to what a person is going to do, or what he thinks, or the state of world affairs, anything . . . these writers should sit and talk to a gang kid for a few hours.

Their eyes say nothing. Their eyes are dying eyes; embers. Despite the carefully-combed pompadour, despite the cutely cruel and insolent droop of the lips, despite the pasty complexions and the cat-jaunty manner, these kids have no souls left to them.

That was what I saw.

I didn't move. I stayed very silent, because I realized, even then, that what was passing me would be the source of my first work in length.

I was then living at 611 West 114th Street, a building between Broadway (so far uptown that the glamour of the name has worn off by the time you've passed Columbus Circle) and Riverside Drive. It had once been a fashionable apartment building, but it had been bought by refugees and the handsome, many-roomed apartments had been cut up to house the down-on-their-luck, the despondent, the college students, the Puerto Ricans without finances, the kooks, and the little old ladies waiting for their monthly government checks and Death.

But it was a good place to live, for all that. It was clean in my room, and I had my typewriter, and in the same building lived Bob Silverberg, who was going to Columbia University, but who was also a writer, and that meant a lot.

I don't think I ever told Bob I was going down to Red Hook to join a gang. I don't think he really knew where I went all those days, and all those nights, appearing only infrequently to check on my mail or push a story to some editor who could provide me with walking-around money.

Because from the day I took that subway out to Stuyvesant Street, till the day I returned and had my hair cut out of the duck's-ass style I affected while with the gang, I was not Harlan Ellison. I was Phil "Cheech" Beldone. I was not twenty-one-year-old Harlan Ellison, originally from Painesville, Ohio, come to New York to make his fortune. I was a seventeen-year-old stud named Cheech who could operate an Italian stiletto without a switch faster than most kids could *with* a switch. I looked seventeen. I acted a hard seventeen, I thought like seventeen. And I lived in Red Hook.

I took a room in Bedford-Stuyvesant, a cheap room for eight bucks a week. A room that was only big enough for me, the radiator clogging the room with heat, a stick-bed, a bureau, a wardrobe, and the bugs. I had different kinds of bugs. I not only had roaches and tenement lice, but I had silverfish in the wallpaper and crab lice in my crotch. It wasn't like that airy, pleasant room uptown across from Columbia University.

It was in a neighborhood near the docks, and it was in a neighborhood that murmured gently of trouble. Flyspecked windows of bars, used clothing stores, appliance shops,

21

bars, malt shops, bars, joints and more joints—and bars. But it was where I wanted to be, for a while.

I wore a pair of blue jeans I'd had for years; jeans I used to wear when I was cleaning the garage back home, or jeans I wore when playing baseball at OSU on a Saturday afternoon. Jeans with holes in them, with the new-looking deep blue worn away, cheap and old and just right for a seventeen-year-old hood without parents living in an eight-buck-a-week coffin in a wall.

I wore an old Merchant Marine survival sweater with a turtle neck. It was three sizes too small for me and made what little chest I had stand out to match the wide yoke of my shoulders. I wore a black leather jacket with shiny-metal stars and studs, and little ball-chains like the ones on key rings, hanging from every one of the zipper pulls. I wore a surplus pair of Army fatigue boots, and I carried tucked down in the top of one of those boots a 12-inch Italian stiletto. I spent hours in my room practicing with that knife, loosening it up so it would spring open at a certain particular flick of my wrist.

I got very good with that knife.

If my book was going to be truth, a kind of truth settlement workers and juvenile authorities could only suspect, I would have to be more than another curious reporter or snoopy youth counselor peering in from the outside. I would have to be one of them. I would have to become a j.d.

So I became a j.d.

For ten weeks Harlan Ellison ceased to exist. For ten weeks it was Cheech Beldone who ran through the parks and streets and over the tenement rooftops of Red Hook.

In those ten weeks I discovered the first part of my story about the lost and the guilty. I learned who these kids were, who they thought they were, who they wanted to be. I learned about what made them nasty, what made them deadly, what doomed them. I learned, also, that they are not—in the main—the sniveling teen-aged punks too often

22

described by paunchy businessmen as "the kind of kids who're yellow; they'd fold up and run if a grown man took a stand in front of them." They were not cowards, and though they ran in packs, they were not a joke. They were killers, and anyone deluding himself into thinking they could be stopped with a spanking, was just as likely to end with a zip gun slug in his forehead.

But I also learned they were not basically bad kids.

They were lonely kids. They were unhappy kids. But they weren't really bad. It sounds trite—Father Flanagan and all that—but these were kids who merely needed a break, a chance, an escape.

They were the children of the gutters, born into a life with no doors, no windows.

They were the lost, not the guilty.

The guilty were the parents. The guilty were the teachers. The guilty were the clergymen. The guilty were the politicians. Everybody and anybody, except those kids. If you disagree, all I can say is: stop bulling yourself and everyone around you: a seventeen-year-old kid doesn't make the System stink. He doesn't like living in filth and poverty and running from the fuzz every time he hears a whistle. Don't fool yourself any longer. The kids are the end-result, the product, the symptoms, not the cause!

You'll see that as you read these pages. But I want you to see much more. I want to take you there and rub your nose in it. I want you to see it the way it has to be seen, from the inside, before it has any validity for you, secure in your nice, warm homes and your nice, warm philosophies. I want you to dig the scene completely; I want you so hip that the next time you read about a Puerto Rican named Angel or Jesus or Chico who has knifed some other kid in a playground, you won't scream *lynch the bastard!* I want you to be so aware of what is going on that you'll want to try to do something to stop the other Angels, or Jesuses, or Chicos, before they get into really bad trouble.

Then I want to take you inside a New York jail, and let you sit on the metal benches with the junkies and the

Oreo queens and the mixed-up kids who don't know their backside from their belly-button. I want you to know their horror of living within the guts of a machine that can take anything fine and good and innocent in even the worst kid criminal, and warp it completely, distort the vessel and turn it back into society more depraved and ready for monstrousness than it ever was before.

This is not the happiest book you'll ever read.

It is a sad but true picture of what things are like, just a little ways beyond your picture window and the Friday night bridge club. It is the way of it, and a way you'll never know unless someone tells you about it. It is the sort of thing P.A.L.—the Police Athletic League—in New York is trying to stop. It is the picture of misery and hopelessness in our country that makes what even the starving West Virginians are going through look like a romp in the countryside. It is so unspeakably brutal and without charm that to tell it any other way would be to gloss it over so as not to offend the finer sensibilities of a nation accustomed to baby food and mush.

You won't find subtleties here.

You won't find niceties.

You won't find shadings or softenings.

That is my obligation to ten weeks of kids who thought I was one of them, and who would have killed me if they'd known I would some day try to wrest them from the squalor and insanity in which they live.

Because, you see, they don't know any other life.

I've cried for them. I want to make *you* cry for them. I want to make you shudder and turn away, and then drag your eyes back to see what a kid looks like, lying there in a gutter with half his face torn away. I want you to know how these kids get their kicks, how they attain status, how they express what passes for love in a society that is loveless, how they feel about their parents, their country, their chances in the world, and even their Gods.

I want you to know them in their moments of truth and their moments of honesty and their moments of warmth

. . . as well as their moments of hate and violence and bitterness.

I want you to know them only half as well as I knew them, and you will realize that good *can* come from evil.

Every time you read the word "I" there must be the identification of yourself as the narrator, walking through the stinking streets of Brooklyn, or clattering down the corridors of a gray, thankless prison. This is a book of sights and sounds, emotions and textures. Truth that does not smell of rosewood and spices.

Perhaps this theme *is* the proper theme: the guilty and the lost. Thousands of kids, dying a little more each day.

And the ones in jails, dying a little more each moment.

The people in this book are real enough, but very often I will not use real names, for that is not part of the bargain. They'll have the names they use in the streets or the cells— Pooch, Fish, Candle, Goofball, Filene, Tooley, Big Teats, Cherry, Angel, Whistler—and that should be enough for you. Just remember that behind each humorous name there is a sad face, a frightened pair of eyes, a lost soul who may have died in Prospect Park or is hooked on H in some Bowery pad or maybe whoring for a living on 42nd Street.

In a larger sense, I have tried to say something about our times, as well as the certain groups who are trapped in it. I have tried to capture a feeling of desperation and corruption that I think is all too common. The lying, the ease with which we steal, cheat and connive . . . the age of the clipster and the fast, hard sell. The turning away from responsibility and action; the toleration of used car salesmen who are expected to rob us, bathroom attendants who would probably wipe our—noses—for a quarter, sin that is double-talked to look like sophistication, insurance claims for phony "whiplash," pistoleros who run labor unions, callousness and rottenness in government, industry, education . . .

All of this is part of the scene, because the sins of the fathers are steadily being deposited on the children, and no one seems to give a damn that we are dying, all of us, every

25

day. We have all become so equal, we have become nothing. We are the Common Man.

In this book I would like to introduce you to that Common Man.

This book tells of two periods in my life: ten weeks in purgatory . . . and 24 hours in hell. Two visits to two different areas of the same dark land. Let me tell you about them.

About the old men and the young men for whom nobody cries.

The guilty, and the lost, written about only in short notes, scribbled phrases on alley walls, messages passed from dirty hands to dirtier hands. Memos from Purgatory.

After *you* . . .

BOOK ONE: THE GANG

CHAPTER ONE

I had to have a job. A good cover, in case there might be suspicion, was mandatory. Perhaps I had been reading too many counter-espionage novels in which T-Men or the like were tripped up by their true identities being revealed to The Bad Guys, perhaps I was being overly melodramatic, and then perhaps what I had seen in the eyes of that bunch of kids on Times Square made me realize I was not playing tot games; these could be very dangerous youngsters. I had to have a job.

Anything steady would hinder my making the scenes whenever I needed to, because for the most part the kids attended school (when they felt like it) and I had to regulate *my* roaming hours with theirs. So I needed part-time work; the money didn't matter too much, because I had a small but satisfactory income from stories being sold by my agent.

I decided dock work would be the best, and so showed up at a dawn "shape-up" in an attempt to get laid on. After half an hour I realized without joining a union I was strictly from Forgetitsville. So regular dock work was out.

But there were enough decent guys shaping for me to inquire and find out that driving a Coca-Cola truck was non-union, and they always needed drivers to service the hold-gangs unloading the ships.

I found out who the licensing outfit was, and asked them for a job. They gave it to me, and I started that day to drive a push-pedal Coke truck around the docks. It was no-think work, and this is the last mention I'll make of it here. I had a name, a job, a pad, and I was ready to try and bust a gang.

That took a bit of doing; it also took a great deal of reconnaissance.

I wandered the neighborhood for almost three days, asking here and there where the kids hung out, if there had been any trouble in the area, who was who and what was what. Eventually, I found a talkative group of Polish and Italian ladies who gossiped on the front steps of a brownstone every afternoon, while airing their sore feet and their tots; no more perfect barometer of neighborhood tensions can be found than the old (and old does not necessarily mean chronologically) women who park their folding tubular-metal chairs on the sidewalk before their homes, and run the block without moving a step.

I grew to know them, began asking discreet questions, and in several hours learned what I needed to know.

A malt shop called Ben's Candy Store had become the hangout of the neighborhood gang. The fellow who ran it, an uncomplicated little Jewish man named Ben Adelstein, had been decent to the kids originally, and that had been his downfall. They had begun congregating there, had requested a juke box (to which request Ben had acquiesced and been under the thumb of the Syndicate juke box boys ever since) and had given him trade. For a faltering neighborhood candy store, the business had been appreciated, but by the time Ben realized he was being used as a hangout, it was too late.

In essence, the kids had taken over the malt shop. It would have done Ben no good to appeal to the beat cops, for he knew the kids—if thwarted—would come back some afternoon or night when the shop was closed, and break every window and backbar mirror he owned. And his business, which had been pale and thin before the advent of the kids, was now wholly dependent upon them. The neighborhood women would not stop in for their afternoon egg cream any longer. He was living off the kids, and so had to put up with their indignities and attentions.

I made a decision to stop in at Ben's that afternoon, when the kids would be out in force.

The shop was narrow across the front, with a long corridor-like section immediately upon entering, opening out into a large square in the rear. Across the left-hand side of the corridor was a soda fountain and candy case, with stools. The right-hand wall was a magazine rack, and in the back was a phone booth, the juke box, a door leading to the stockroom and the back alley, and eight enclosed booths for seated couples.

I surveyed the place from across the street in an all-night Laundromat, and when I saw more than a dozen kids enter the shop, knew it was almost time for my grand entrance. It was a very testy business; I had to get myself in with them, but not alarm them. I had to gain their trust, and hadn't the vaguest idea how I'd do it.

I looked like one of their crowd ... same age ... same easily identifiable status symbols (the hair d.a., the black jacket, the boots, the insolent curl to the lips) ... but a newcomer was always suspect, always had to prove himself.

I pushed open the front door of the Laundromat and started across the sidewalk. Somehow my eyes grew toward the front of Ben's Malt Shop, and every detail of the place was burned into memory. Trucks passed across my line of vision and were only momentary blurs as I advanced, step after step. It was as though the store-front was the only thing in this life, and I had to remark on every facet before it was too late.

There was a large plate glass window, silled in wood that was oily brown and decaying. The window was dark with fly-leavings, the faint patina of soot that could never really be cleaned from a New York window, and an absence of light from within. It was almost a mud-brown, with the words Ben's Malt Shop on it, beginning to peel away the silver with black edges. There was a 7-Up decal near the lower right hand corner of the window, and an El Producto decal, and a half dozen other signs and metal plates either Scotch taped or stuck in otherwise manners to the inside of the glass. The entire window was covered by a metal grating, almost like the wire fences surrounding schoolyards.

I have no idea why I noted this all so completely. Perhaps I felt I was entering a cave of terror and might never again emerge. Whatever it was, as that building grew larger in my sight, I noted the striped, faded awning, rolled up above the window; the metal machinery for lowering that awning when a sprocketed pole was inserted in the turnpost.

I was across the street now, and how I had avoided being hit by the great, lumbering produce trucks that snarled along the cobblestones, I'll never know.

The door had the numbers in gold decals (peeling) near the top, and almost at eye-level a small cartoon figure—product-image, I suppose—of a child with blonde hair, clutching a bottle of Squirt. There was an L&M decal and another El Producto emblem on the glass, and a pull-handle with a lock attached. I could make out dim figures in the store.

At that moment I had a terrible feeling of wanting to turn and run. A feeling of something almost like history, though now when I think about it, the feeling seems ludicrous. But at that moment I knew I was going on, could not turn back, and it frightened me.

I pulled open the door and walked inside Ben's.

The stools along the left-hand side of the room were filled. But the kids were not turned toward the counter. On the contrary, they had their backs braced against the marble counter-edge, were slouched across the stools, and had their feet pressed flat against the opposite wall, just under the wooden magazine racks nailed there. Long black slide

32

marks on the wall indicated this was their traditional position, and they had done it many times before, scuffing their soles down the wall when they got up. It was, in effect, a perfect barricade of legs. No one could pass unless he either shoved their legs away, allowing passage, or waited for them to drop feet.

Simple. Perfect. A test of guts and spunk for whoever entered the shop.

In the space of a second I took in the ten or eleven sets of legs, and the frightened, harried-looking little man behind the counter pouring milk into a metal milk-shake tin, and the girls sitting on the stools, and the couples in the back dancing—despite the absence of a cabaret license that permitted dancing.

The juke box was playing something by Fats Domino. It stank. The entire place, for that matter, had the faint reek of tension and kids waiting for something to happen.

I made out the dim brown bulk of the telephone booth at the back, and decided my excuse for having entered the place was to make a phone call.

I took a breath, no deeper than usual, but a good deal more important at that moment than any other breath had ever been, and moved forward toward the first pair of barricading legs. I was not going to stop.

He was a tall boy, and most of his height was in those terribly-braced legs right in front of me. He had a shock of oily black hair, and a curl that hung down carelessly, Sal Mineo-style, across his forehead. His eyes were almost like bits of coal, or little raisins, thrust into the doughy white mass of his face. But he wasn't fat. His face was white, almost cadaverous, and even more brilliantly-highlighted by the hollows in his cheeks, the dark splotches under his black eyes. He stared at me, sizing me, the way they say it "making me," as I advanced steadily on him. Just at that split-instant before I would have to hit his legs away, or hip-shove through them (but in the same instant he knew I would not back down), he dropped them.

It was a signal to all the others. As I moved down the

line, everyone watching me, silence now save for the nasal twanging of Fats Domino alone in the juke box, each pair of blue-jeaned or chino-covered legs dropped with a clank against the counter.

The last person was a girl, slouched back on the stool so that her breasts became painfully apparent against the yellow wool of her sweater. She was not a particularly good looking girl, but there was a heavy sensuousness, an Italian langour, on her petulant lips, in her deep eyes, in the fine texture of her cheekbones and eye-socket ridges. I was later to find out she was Anybody's Girl (as they called her in WEST SIDE STORY), that she had been balled by every stud in the gang, and was looked on more as a chattel than a human being. But this status was something that was hers, hers only, all hers. She had become a hard, chippie-like female, ready to smart-mouth or slap anyone who buzzed her.

I walked up to her legs and she tightened them at the knees, making them harder to knock down. Her skirt rode above her knees, on the lower, less-fleshy part of her thighs. She smiled at me insolently.

Without really knowing what I was doing, I stopped.

"Goin' back, Big Man?" she asked. It seems peculiarly adolescent and false-to-the-ears now, but at that time, in that fraction of a moment when my getting the hell beaten out of me rested with what she said and how I replied, it had all the import and significance of the world's greatest exit lines.

I leered back at her with what I hoped was adolescent bravado, and shoved her legs straight away—rather than down—spinning her on the stool so she almost lost her seat.

"I stopped pickin' green apples like you when I was twelve," I snapped, and without looking at her, walked quite steadily past the empty space between the corridor and the open square back room, past the booths with their staring-at-me occupants, past the juke box and into the phone booth.

Reflex took the dime from my jeans' watch-pocket; reflex put the dime in the slot; reflex held my right index finger over the receiver hook as I put the receiver to my ear. Reflex dialed the nonsensical number.

I was breathing like a deer run halfway cross-country. The sweat that lived in my armpits, the spine down my back, my palms, my upper lip was something too cold to think about. All I could say to myself was *Jesus, Jesus, Jesus, that was as close as I ever want to get. Oh Jesus!*

With the booth door accordioned shut I could hear very little from the malt shop beyond, but even if there had been no door closed, I was so after-the-fact paralyzed I wouldn't have heard anything in any case.

Finally, when my mouth moistened and my knees (behind my knees, actually) grew calm, I replaced the receiver, pocketed the dime that had clinked back, its clink covered by my hurried dialing, and left the booth.

As I emerged from the booth, I heard someone laughing, and someone else saying, "Man, he plugged *your* hole, Flo!"

Then they were all laughing.

They had been laughing for some minutes.

I was only later to learn that Flo had seldom been put down completely by her associates; that I was one of the first strangers who had ever bucked her. (I attribute this to stupidity on my part, hardly bravery.) She was a private joke among them; someone they felt close to, but who was the brunt of jokes. I had struck a common denominator; I had hit a proper chord. It could easily have gone either way, but they had laughed, rather than taken offense.

No one was glaring at me. No one was angry. I was a tolerated visitor in the enemy camp.

I walked up to Flo, who was crimson with rage at being put down, and smiled at her boyishly. I hoped it was even engagingly. "Sorry," I grinned, meaning that I was not sorry but if she'd call it square, so would I.

She turned away spinning on the stool with an indignant

exhalation of breath, that peculiar expression without words or motions that means get the hell away from me, big mouth, I'm insulted.

Everyone was laughing.

I had to cement my place among them, tenuous though it might be.

Clichés *are* clichés because they're true. They work. I employed as simple a cliché as I could dream up on the spur of the moment. "Hey," I called to the white-around-the-eyes frightened Ben, "give everybody a Coke on me."

Set 'em up for the house, bartender.

It was so trite, it was so hokey, it was so pure and simple a grandstand play, it got carried off flawlessly. I bought them Cokes, and they didn't mind when I took Flo's seat as she left the malt shop in anger and frustration.

They talked to me sparingly, not telling me their names, and myself refraining from asking. They did not tell me what club they belonged to, what they did, where they went, nothing. I was still a stranger. They didn't ask me about myself, and I didn't tell them.

We talked about inconsequentialities. Ball games, movies, the street cleaners, the cops, the stores around, records on the juke box, whether Coke or Pepsi was better, that a piece of meat left overnight in a glass of Coke was eaten by the acid, a lot of crap like that, as they phrased it.

But I was talking with them, and whether they knew it or not, they had a new member in their gang.

It was a feeling that knotted me inside like a length of hemp rope. I was about to get involved more deeply with trouble than I had ever been before.

These kids played hard, and they lived hard, and they were jealous of their lives. They wanted no interference, no interlopers, no prying youth counselors. If they knew I was a busy-body writer gathering their expressions, the absent movements of their hands when they spoke, their facial expressions, they would stomp and slice me like a pound of salami.

36

I tried talking to them about current events, mentioned some local governmental disturbance. They thought I was a kook. I got off that kick and recouped my conversational losses and learned a lesson, my first about the gang kids:

They lived in a private world. A teen-aged universe outside adults and adult matters. Their world was the turf—their neighborhood, their territory, the blocks they ruled—and sputniks, revolutions, United Nations, strikes and depressions were of no interest to them, did not, in effect, exist for them. They lived in the malt shop, on the doorstep, on the rooftop, in the parked car, on the dance floor, and other worlds were not their concern.

This was their kingdom, and anyone wanting admission had to think like them, act like them, be like them.

I never made that slip-up again.

From the moment I raised that valuable Coke to my lips, I was a seventeen-year-old hood named Cheech Beldone, and if they killed a druggist while robbing his till, or knocked down old ladies in the park, or if they zip-gunned a rival gang member, I was with them.

I had to write the truth, and that meant no play-acting.

It meant living the life of the doomed.

I *was* a hard rock j.d. from that moment on.

CHAPTER TWO

I had been coming into Ben's nearly a week before they decided to ask me to join the gang.

By that time I had learned a few superficial facts: the club's name was The Barons, they were one of the five largest gangs in Brooklyn, the members were all between the ages of sixteen and twenty (though there was apparently some sort of "junior" group for apprentice toughs), and nearly all were of Central European extraction, principally Polish, Hungarian, German and Italian, with several Irish or Scotch extractions tossed in at random.

I had been watching myself carefully, and had sunk so deeply into the "Method" of my role that I sometimes found it difficult to think of myself as never having lived in this restless, humid world of tension and breathless expectancy.

It was the first really startling revelation of my time in the gang to learn that there was really no glamour attached to their way of life. No wild rides across rain-wet streets in stolen cars, no Douglas Fairbanks forays into enemy gang turf ... nothing but a waiting. Waiting. Always waiting. For something to happen. For someone to make a move, or offer a means of diversion. Boredom. Ennui. The waiting. Hurry up and hurry up, but nothing else at the end of the time. Just waiting. On front stoops. On rooftops. In candy stores. On street corners. On park benches. Just waiting. Waiting.

Time choked them slowly, drawing juices from their bodies. And still they waited. Nervously twisting.

At the end of the first week I knew they were interested in me. I had struck up semi-friendships with several of the boys, chiefly with the arrogant-looking tall boy who had been first in line on the leg-barricade.

His gang-name was Pooch, or sometimes Poochie, and he was the leader of the gang, the President, the Prez. If a guy was down that week, if he had goofed or had made a pass at someone else's chick, he was close-mouthed by the rest of the gang, put in Coventry, and he called Poochie by the formal "Prez." I called him Pooch; I was not in the gang. The loss of familiarity is extended or pressed upon only those who have known the familiarity first.

But it was not only the tentative conversational feelers Pooch and the others put out that led me to believe they were interested in me as a recruit. I had seen several of the guys hanging around the docks where I worked, asking questions once in a while, but usually just leaning against a bale or a packing crate or a piling: they'd been asking about me.

Watching.

Watching me. Making me with their cold, seeing eyes.

And someone had checked on where I lived.

I did not go back to Manhattan and my real pad during that time. I hung the streets, shot some pool from time to time, bought a few paperbacks and read them, wandered in and out of movies, killed time. Waiting.

How easy it was to become spiritually one of them. How easy. How damned deadly easy.

Finally, one afternoon, almost a week to the day later, I was sipping a chocolate Coke in Ben's, when Pooch and his Vice-President, a painfully thin boy with acne, named Fish, busted me on the subject of joining.

"Hey!" they enjoindered me, sliding onto stools on either side. I dipped my head in greeting as Fish spun

39

around, stretching his elbows back to rest on the counter, putting his booted feet on the wall.

"What's shakin'?" I asked.

Pooch pursed his lips and nodded his head, a peculiar expression of everything being *just fine, man, just fine.* It was a silent okay, a silent acceptance, a thing very hard to describe, but not very easy to forget in its eloquence.

"We, uh, we been talkin'," Fish started, "we been talkin' to some of the men an' they, well, they been talkin' to us—"

He screwed it up badly. He had probably asked Pooch for the honor of asking me, and had muffed it. Now Pooch motioned him to shut his mouth, and the Prez leaned in toward me. Nothing changed in the store, but though everyone else went on dancing or shooting the bull, I knew all eyes were on us, all ears tuned in to what we were saying.

"You don't belong to a club, do ya?" Pooch asked. He knew damned well I didn't. I was too new in the neighborhood. I shook my head.

"Well, look, we uh we got a club, see, and we told you about it from time to time, you know, The Barons, and some of us got together and you were put up at the last meeting Wednesday, Wednesday night. We wanted to know would you like to be a member, because in our turf nobody walks unless'n he's a member, you know, you unnerstand what I mean?"

I understood perfectly.

In Baron turf, you were either with us or against us.

If you were an eligible chick, you either belonged to the Barons' girls' auxiliary, the Baron Debutantes, or Debs—or you didn't go out alone. If you were a guy, you either belonged, or risked your can every time you went down to buy a pack of cigarettes or catch a flick. You were either a recognized Baron, in good standing...or they didn't leave you standing.

The locusts of Brooklyn, sweeping all before them.
Even the adults knew; even the fuzz, the cops, knew.
What choice did I have, had I wanted a choice?
Join—or get bombed.

"Hey, that's great. Yeah, I wouldn't mind joinin', you know, dependin' on what's what and who is and who ain't."

Pooch nodded his head. He was satisfied with the answer. He jammed a finger lightly against my bicep. "Listen, t'night you be down here about what? about eight-thirty, and we'll send one of the guys for you. If you want to join up and swear allegiance, then we can have the initiation t'night, an' tomorrow you're a Baron, howzabout?"

"Wild," I replied, and went back to my Coke, shaking inside like a vibrator gone berserk.

They split, leaving me to sip my Coke.

Ben looked at me with pity. Little did he know, poor old Ben Adelstein.

I made the scene at exactly eight-thirty, cruising the block for ten minutes to insure my appearance at exactly the half-hour mark. Another of the gang kids I had seen and talked to briefly during the past week, a short four-teen-year-old everyone called Shit (chiefly because he was the errand-boy, the smallest member of the gang, a hang-er-on), was waiting for me.

He was a pathetic kid, more like the pictures of Jackie Coogan as "The Kid" than anything else I could name. His nose was constantly running, there were always scrape marks and scabs on the exposed portions of his body, and he wore a dirty sailor's hat that had been so often twisted in nervous fingers it was wrinkled and pressed almost out of its original shape. But he was apparently reliable, and so they let him remain in the gang, despite the fact that he was—simply—Shit, to them.

I wish I had a buck for every time someone banged him around, just for chuckles.

"I'se waitin' to take you over," he grinned at me, with-

41

out realizing he was grinning. He was trying desperately to be stern and secretive about this; Secret Agent X-9 on a vital mission. But the sad little puppy-dog of him was so pleased to be able to attain any status at all, even running such a nothing errand, it worked the smile muscles of his face.

I didn't grin back at him. That wasn't cool, to smile back at a nowhere kid like him. "Let's go," I said.

We left Ben's, and almost immediately took to the back alleys. It wasn't really necessary, but Shit must have felt it was more mysterious to lead me five blocks away, through alleys, to a condemned building, than to walk the streets like normal people.

Alleys become a way of life, eventually.

We finally made the tenement, and dropped down through the bent-together struts of a grate that had been bolted over the mouth of the service entrance. There were four steps, now completely littered with garbage sacks half-rotted away, cat and dog offal, old cigarette packs sticky with rain moisture, anything and everything a callous urban population throws into its streets. The building had been condemned a year before, had never been pulled down, and so the jungle-like encroachment of waste and disregard of the city and its people had begun to eat at the structure. Rats nested in the building, soot and dirt bit chips from its sills and adornments, rust pitted the front door frames, windows got broken ... and gang kids used it as a club house.

Walking inside the body of a metropolitan corpse.

We took the service alley to its end, and the kid knocked in a counter-intelligence manner, involved and too difficult to bother remembering. The splintered green door opened and one of the Debs stood back to let us pass.

The kid walked ahead of me, through the dusky, as-phalt-floored basement. I saw a stand of filthy wash basins for laundry on one wall. Behind us, the girl slammed the door and slipped a bolt easily enough to tell me it was new, that it had been installed by the Barons. Organization.

Shit walked me through four medium-sized basement rooms without doors; apparently storage areas when the building had been inhabited. The darkness was not complete: every room had a candle in a bottle burning, casting grotesque and flickering bluish-grey shadows across the dirty asphalt floor and the walls of naked brick.

Finally, we came out into a corridor (apparently the linkage between the janitorial areas and the sub-residential sections of the building) and at the end of the passage I could see a large door, freshly painted a blood-red.

Someone had very neatly lettered

KNOCK BEFORE ENTERING

on the wooden face of the door, and below it a wise guy had scrawled, *This means you!* That was not the end of the quotation; the ! was replaced by a curse word involving a strange juxtapositioning of the head and the anus. It didn't do a thing for the semantics of the door.

The kid repeated his special knock, and I could hear a great deal of scuffling and moving around from within, as though the cast were preparing for the curtain to rise.

When the door opened I was staring directly into a blazing light. Somehow they had tapped a power line and were drawing juice down into the basement club rooms; the light into which I was staring was a klieg, a huge theatrical lamp with a golden gel on its face, and the damned thing was directly in my eyes.

It was like staring into the sun.

"C'mon in," Shit urged me, pulling me by the edge of my sweater (a small dog worrying a large bone into its sanctum). I slapped his hand away, cursing at the top of my lungs, "Turn that effin' thing off before I put a fist through it!"

The raucous, guttural jibes of a dozen voices came back at me from the golden halo surrounding the light. "Oh,

43

wow! *Tough man . . . real tough . . . stud, stud stuffin'
stud . . ."*

I had shielded my eyes immediately after the first blast
of light had struck them, but to all intents and purposes I
was stone-blind. I struggled forward into the room, and a
pair of hands whirled me around. I heard the door slam
and bolt behind me.

"Hey hey hey hey hey HEY!" half a dozen of them
were jeering now, and I felt myself shoved from one to
another. It was a harrying, a chivvying, and it was the beginning of my initiation. If I'd expected a somber, re-
strained adolescently-pompous ceremony, it was now a
foolish expectation.

They tossed me around like a metal bearing in a pinball
machine, and every time I dropped my hands from my
eyes to swing on someone, I caught another, fresh blast
from that damned klieg light. I had a whirling quick-
thought that whatever theatrical shop they'd pilfered to
get that light would never think of its being used this way.

Then I was volley-balled around the room again, and
some sonofabitch took a clip at my head and stung me
across the ear. I cursed like a longshoreman and swung
out. My elbow cracked into somebody's shoulder and I
heard the kid curse me as a ratbastard, and then they
dribbled me a while longer.

Finally, when my legs were starting to act like someone
else's, I heard Pooch commanding, "Okay, lay off. That's
enough. C'mon, you creeps, let 'im alone!"

I was suddenly by myself in a golden fog of blindness,
and I spread my fingers slightly to see if I was still staring
into the light. Who could tell? *Everything* was still yellow
flickering coruscating golden, with a wow-wow-wow like
reverberations of light.

My eyes felt burned.

But somebody maneuvered me to a seat, and I plopped
down. In a few minutes I knew the effects of that light
would wear off, but for now, even if they had turned it
off, I was a cripple.

There was a subterranean undercurrent of voices, very much like that of an operating room, the gallery filled with young students and interns; like that of a study hall in a high school; like that of a baseball park in that fractional instant between the time the pitcher has thrown the ball and it reaches the plate. It was silence with sound.

My eyes were watering from my having squeezed them with my fingers. I could feel the sensation of sight coming back, though, and I blinked, removing my hands. The light was out; the room was lit by candles in Chianti bottles. It was a lousy effect, particularly with the sprinkled red and yellow and deep-blue and black circles that bobbed and capered in front of my eyes.

"Very funny," I said, sarcastically, to no one in particular. There was a rising titter of laughter.

"Well, listen, goddammit, one of you smart bastards wanna step in here and laugh, I'll kick the crap out of you!" I wasn't acting; I was madder than hell! I would have done it.

Pooch's voice came from the right of me, and my head swivelled at the sound. "Okay, don't get wise, *recruit!*"

That one word pulled me out of my anger. It was all a part of the game, I had to remember that. I had to remember what I was in this basement to do, what I had to learn, and so I had to play their kid game, because I was a kid. I settled back, pursing my lips to stop the remarks I wanted very much to make.

As my eyes cleared I could make out the room more clearly; oddly colorful in the fitful glare of the candles. The walls had been painted jaunty colors—or insane colors, if one looked at it from another point of view. Huge swaths of crimson, great blotches of robin's egg blue, smears and dollops of yellow. It was a riot of completely unartistic color-forms; someone's half-baked idea of what an artist's pad would have for walls. Or had they merely taken turns and part-times slapping it on?

The ceiling was lost in a smoky greyness, and whatever its color, they had left it dark to make the ceiling seem lower. So low did it seem, in fact, that there was a claustrophobic tightness to the room, despite the mad mash of colors on the walls.

There were no windows. We were below street level.

Someone had bought, borrowed or liberated a rattan mat for a rug, and it stretched all across the floor of the huge room, and rolled like a window shade against the far wall. I suspected some storekeeper with a huge front window was minus a curtain.

They had retrieved items of overstuffed furniture from refuse piles left for pick-up outside the larger apartment buildings, and the room was tastelessly furnished in Period Squalor. Great spring-thrusting Morris chairs, a down-at-the-legs sofa without cushions, a sling chair that had been slung once too often. Packing crates and old orange cartons did yeoman duty where chairs and tables could not be found. One girl sat cross-legged on an ottoman, her skirt forming a tent that showed at a glance she wore no underwear. The lamps were all, strangely enough, brand new, and it ceased confusing me as I realized how easy it was to swipe a lamp from a ten cent store or furniture shop; lamps are designed for easy theft.

There was a bar, of sorts, on one corner, and I was mildly surprised to see half a dozen cases of Budweiser stacked beside it. Again, theft from beer trucks was relatively simple, in the land of the tots.

There were pictures on the walls.

Playboy is a favorite in the hung-up set. Also *Man's Hairy-Chested Adventures Magazine*, able as it is to furnish four-color illustrations for stories titled, "I Was Eaten Alive By Army Ants," or "The Killer Buffalo Gored My Guts!" It was not the first time I was to realize these kids had an unquenchable capacity for violence of the most drunken sort, nor was it the last, by any means ... but it was one of the most impressive.

The room was filled. Though the entire gang was not present (and none of the juniors were allowed) there must have been at least thirty boys and half as many girls. It was a big night. It was a social function. It was my initiation night, and so ring out the sparklers and bunting.

Again Pooch spoke out over the low hum of interested watchers. He spoke like a clergyman intoning a solemn message, the way the scoutmaster spoke when you won your Eagle badge beside the campfire, the way your father spoke when he told you what girls were for. It was a serious matter, and he wasn't fooling around.

"What is your name, *recruit?*"

I didn't even think about my answers. I let my reflexes and my synapses and my gonads work for me. "Phil Beldone."

"How old are you, *recruit?*"

"Seventeen."

"You ever belonged to a rival gang or enemy club in any other turf besides this one?"

"No."

"Are you a Jew or a nigger or a communist?"

It was easy to lie about the first, and I didn't have to worry about the second and third. "No."

"Do you want to become a member in good standing in the club called the Barons?"

"Yes."

"Why?"

"Because ... because I live here and I want to, uh, because I want to join a good club, that's all."

There was a moment's silence. I could have given them a half hour polemic on why I wanted to join their damned club, but it was no great tactical decision to play illiterate: When in Rome ...

In the kingdom of the blind, the one-eyed man is King.

"Do you promise to uphold all the commandments and rules and regulations of this club if you are accepted?"

"Yes."

"Will you give your life for the club or any of its brother members or Debs?"

"Uh, yes, yeah."

47

"Do you recognize the authority of the President and the other officers in all things?"

I was getting impatient with all this phony ritual crap. "Sure, yeah!"

"And are you prepared to undergo the initiation all members of the Barons have to undergo?"

Oh boy, I thought, *here goes my lunch . . .*

"Yeah," I said.

"Okay, men, he's all yours," Pooch said, fading back.

I turned my head in the direction he'd spoken, and there they were, big as life——and farewell to my own:

Six cats as big as houses, stripped to the gut and garrison belts wrapped around their hands. The buckles were as sharp as razors. It was pay day.

CHAPTER THREE

It took four guys to get my sweater and T-shirt off me. I kicked one of them squarely in the groin and another in the shin and stomped on another one's instep, and used my free elbow in the throat of another one, and it did no good at all. The four of them stripped me to the waist, forcing me down on my knees between them, and one kid holding my neck so tightly I thought the s.o.b. would cut off my wind completely. Two of them held my arms behind me, straight out with one guy hunched over, his knee in the small of my back. I was contorted like the India rubber man, and they weren't being particularly gentle with me, either.

Suddenly it was no longer research.

Abruptly, I was not Stanley, presumably, the reporter, or Ernie Pyle, or Hemingway, or anydamnbody but me, and I was scared witless. These weren't kindergarten rompers playing pranks. These were teen-aged kids with more muscles than they had any right to have, bending me down like a sapling in a storm and ripping the clothes off me.

I wanted out of there.

No one will ever know how hard I wanted out of there.

I tried to yell at them, something logical and complete and round and tight like a ball bearing, something that would make them let go of my windpipe and my back (which was breaking) and let me bolt the hell out of there.

But I had said I wanted in, and that was the way it was going to be. If it killed me.

Crazy thoughts skimmed through my mind.

I won't relate them here, they don't count; I was half crazy with fear. Except that I really wanted out.

When they had the clothes off me, they shoved me away, and I went to my hands, as well as my knees. Instinctively I knew if I'd come this far, there were only two courses open to me. The first was to break and run and get rudely (if cadaverously) ejected from the turf; the second was to suck in my yellow streak and tough it out. I'm no braver than the next one, but six guys with belt buckles honed to razor sharpness were a pretty authoritative fighting force, and there was no telling how far they'd go. Bluff? Maybe? But there were a good many kids with scars across their faces, and their backs a tanned plane criss-crossed with white lines—scars—where the sun would never tan them. They might be knife wounds from rumbles, but on the other hand they might be belt buckle momentos.

Pooch decided for me.

"Get in line, you guys, c'mon, he's goin' through; get in *line,* willya for Chrissakes!"

They lined up, Indian gantlet style. All across the long room, about six feet apart, three on each side, alternately spaced diagonally across from each other perhaps seven feet. It was as deadly a row as I'd ever seen a guy have to hoe.

"What are you outta your goddam *mind?*" I yelled to Pooch. "I didn't come down here to get my ass stripped off!"

"Either run or fold," he said.

It was as simple as that.

I knew what I was going to do.

But I had to do it right. Just right.

"No dice. To hell with you!" I said, half turning away, as though looking for the way out. They lowered the belts for an instant, and—

—I jumped like a scared rabbit and hit that gantlet going full blast before they knew I was coming. I got past three of them before they knew I was coming, and skimmed under a side-arm slash by the tallest kid, even as the ones I'd passed howled, *"Foul!"*

The fifth one was slightly smaller than the others, and he swung his big black belt in a wide S curve that I felt whistle past my back with barely an inch clearance. The sixth one was waiting, and he was grinning like Eichmann with a fresh furnace-load ready to be basted. I knew I'd never get past him. That bastard would level me with one swipe, probably open my skull or slit my throat or slice my back to the bone. I *knew* I'd never make it.

I ducked sidewise, broken-field style, and grabbed the fifth one, the smaller one, around the waist, before he could draw back for another swing. I carried that fink on ahead of me with the force of my rush like he was a heavy load of kindling, and I hurled him into the sixth cat with all my might.

They went bumbling together, the belt caught the fifth guy across the shoulders and he howled as though some-one had rammed a poker up his backside, and I was through the gantlet, panting like a steam engine, but clear and clean.

A couple of them started after me, and I crouched down, ready to hit the first one with everything in me, if he brought that belt up . . . but Pooch called time.

"Cool it!" he yelled across the room. We were in the shadows, and I was all Floyd Pattersoned to roundhouse the first creep that stuck his face within range. "C'mon, knock it off you guys, he made it . . ."

And I had, too.

Round one of The Initiation of Cheech Beldone was over.

There was a mild demonstration, at that point, chiefly

51

from the Debs sitting on the tables and orange crates. Doug Fairbanks had come through once more.

But I could tell I'd made a few enemies; there were kids in that group who were too chicken to fight it out in an open stand; they were the ones who *had* to prowl in groups, because they were afraid of getting caught alone, of laying their courage on the line. They were the ones with the deadly cruel little eyes, and the hard sets to their mouths (that became soft and white when they thought no one was watching). They got their kicks from organized brutality, and I'd robbed them of their kicks. Therefore I was a fink, and an enemy.

I could tell at once who they were. There were three of them. I marked them mentally, for watching. Never a back turned toward them. Never.

Yet I'd made it through the gantlet.

I thought the initiation was over.

I was wrong.

"You got two more parts to the initiation," Pooch announced. They all knew it, but I hadn't. I was too beat and too scared to realize what he was saying, but after a few moments I let it filter through, and my blood went dry in my veins. I wasn't sure I could take two more tests of endurance like the one I'd just come through.

I suddenly had a vision of some poor little *schmuck* like Fish or Shit trying to make that gantlet. Yet I knew they must have, for they were in the gang, and I was only one-third of the way there. (I later found out the initiation rites were highly flexible; and that up until six months before I'd joined the gang, there had been hardly any initiation at all . . . merely a ritual of talking.)

I took in all the faces, and the looks on their faces made them something other than faces. They were masks, like the *Comedia del' Arte*; representations, rather than realities. They were a Roman Circus audience, waiting for a martyr to meet his lion.

They were a carny crowd waiting for the aerialist to take his dive, and kill himself. They wanted blood. They

52

wanted to turn thumbs down on this particular gladiator, no matter who he was; they wanted blood.

"Well, come on, what's next?" I demanded.

It was getting to me, now. I was becoming light-headed and weak from the sprint and tackle through the gantlet; what the next part might be, I had no idea, *but it had better be non-strenuous,* I thought, wryly.

"Pick a chick," Pooch ordered. He made a negligent half-wave at the girls sitting around the room. There was no room for misunderstanding; he was telling me I was going to ball one of the gang Debs—either in full sight of the rest of them, or in private. But either way, I was now about to prove my masculinity to the group.

I cast a wide, slow look around the room. I knew, roughly, which girls belonged to certain studs. I also knew certain *other* girls—Flo was one of them—who were considered below-status for any sort of steady dating or affection, but who were perfectly acceptable for balling. But that wasn't the sort of chick I was being ordered to pick.

This was a test in many ways. They were gauging my good judgment, my critical sense, my coolness, in fact. I had to pick a good-looking girl who was not a bum, who was not strongly attached to any club member, who wouldn't give me a hard time, but who would carry into her sexual meet with me all the qualities of a "good" girl, yet be hip enough to make me a steady chick.

I was, in effect, picking a gang-wife.

Of the fifteen or sixteen girls in the basement room, only five were known to me to be in the category—that tenuous, unspoken category—from which I would be wise to select.

There was a dishwater blonde named Midget (nickname derived from the size of her bosom) with whom I'd talked on several occasions. She liked me; I'd informed her it was my habit to call "dishwater" blondes, "sunshine" blondes, and one of God's most attractive creatures. It was a great deal of snow, but she liked me. Her legs were very thin.

Pam and Lou were friends, went to the same school,

lived in the same tenement, and generally double-dated; both were moderately attractive, in that flashy, too-tight-looking way teen-aged girls look these days. Lou wore her hair back in a pony-tail, which became her; her hair was as black as any shadow in that room. Pam was a brownette, but she'd done a few tricks with bleach, and had a streak of blonde incongruously snaking through the mouse-brown. Both were abundantly endowed, and both were taller than me.

Lights was the fourth girl, and she was out of the question. Not that she wasn't good-looking, because if a person's taste happens to run to the Coleen Gray-type girl, with thin, heart-shaped face, pointed nose and slim mouth, then she was, indeed, good-looking. My taste happened to run in other directions. Lights . . . was out. My taste ran.

It ran in the direction of the fifth girl, Filene, who was slim and about a foot shorter than myself, with fine, long fingers and a carriage far more graceful than any of the other girls in the neighborhood sported. She had somehow failed to pick up the hideous habit of scuffling her feet as she walked, a trait common to almost every other teen-aged girl I'd ever encountered, and particularly prevalent in the Baron Debs. She did not chew gum, her complexion was clear, she spoke gently, almost musically, *when* she spoke, and I had a flitting hunch she was a virgin.

Which was probably why none of the other studs had gone for her. They were used to getting their bed-action without too much fuss and nonsense, and her näive purity stood out in that room like a light in the forest. She was in that class of girls known to easily-awed kids of the streets as "high-class."

Her mother worked as a seamstress in the garment center of Manhattan, her father was a neighborhood hanger-on who did odd jobs, hauled ashes, drank sneaky pete and in general kept out of everyone's way, except for the nights he'd scoot back to their apartment and try to seduce Filene. Failing that, he would rough up and ball his wife with a thoroughness that was legend in the turf.

And somehow, she had come through it all reasonably untouched.

"I'll take Filene," I said.

There were great animal grins from all around the room, and I saw the girl pale noticeably. So that was it. This was as much an initiation for her as for me; she'd known it was to come some time, and she had no idea whether I'd be kind or a slob, as so many of the others had been. I knew for certain, then, that she was a virgin.

"You get that room over there," Pooch pointed, and for the first time I saw a door between two highboys. I moved toward it, and she joined me.

I had learned another lesson about morality in the gangs:

There was unbelievable laxity in the morality of the kids, but it was still tied up inextricably with the mores of the times. It was all right to ogle a naked photo of Jayne Mansfield, but it was not all right to ball your chick in sight of a bunch of grinning brother gang-members. It was okay to knock a chick up, as long as you did it on the sly, and only talked about it with adolescent braggadocio. It was permissible to get a little in the drive-in theatre, but on the street you don't hold hands. It was fine to rough up a guy's sister in the vestibule of their building, but not a word could anyone say about *your* sister. Mothers were sacrosanct to the words of anyone else, even if Moms was a tosspot lush with a thirst bigger than her brain. You could do anything at all, sexually, under cover, but it wasn't decent to make it in public.

Orgies, mixed couples balling in the same room, sex with the lights on . . . all of it was taboo.

Filene moved toward me, and I opened the door. I went through first; it wasn't a mark of strength to let a Deb precede you *anywhere*—even to her defloration.

I closed the door behind me.

The room said one thing: You're here to make it.

There wasn't a chair, a table, a washstand, a picture, a

rug, a window, wallpaper, *anything* in that cell of horror. There was only a bed.

Filene stood across the room, her eyes invisible in the darkness, but I knew they were wide with expectation and fear. I heard her move, rather than seeing her, and the bed springs creaked as she sat down. I walked to the spot where I thought the end of the bed must be, and reached out. It wasn't there. I moved forward till my hand touched the brass footboard. I could hear her breathing, deeply, regularly.

Okay, so there it was.

I had a choice. Either go all the way, and *be* Cheech Beldone, and get through this initiation, and write my book and forget I'd committed statutory rape ... or fake out of it somehow and run the risk that every girl in that room had been briefed to report what happened in here, and if I didn't come through as was expected they would either bounce me from the gang, or start to suspect something was wrong.

After all, I *was* a perfectly normal, sex-hungry seventeen-year-old gang recruit. If I didn't make it with Filene, she might be grateful as all hell, but I'd be tagged a kook, or worse, intolerably in that set, a homosexual. I didn't really have much choice.

I moved around the bed. She stopped breathing for a long moment. "How old are you?" I asked.

"Sixteen," she said. How softly.

"Jeezus," I snorted, "Whyn't I pick somebody who knew what was happening?" I got up and moved across the room, slouched against the wall. I was scared worse than her.

"I'mmm sssorryy," she drew the words out, humming them, almost, as though they were impregnated with tears even as spoken.

"Forget it," I said, "it isn't your fault."

We both knew what we were talking about, though neither of us had mentioned it.

"Listen, I—uh—I don't mind. If it was Fish or Wally or

Tarzan I wouldn't like it at all, but you don't look like them kids at all." It was the most pathetic rationalization I'd ever heard. I wanted to get out of there *immediately!*

"Listen," she said again, that pathetic twist in her voice, "I'm sorta in bad with them, too. I been in the Debs almost six months now and they, uh, they haven't, I mean nobody's—"

She left it hanging. What she was trying to say was *They're getting impatient with my holding out. I've got to give it to someone and if it's going to you, please be gentle, please be kind. Please.*

How do you equate morality, ethics, good or bad—in a pitch-black basement room with nothing but a bed and a pretty girl?

Sometimes the right things get done for the wrong reasons, and sometimes the wrong things get done for the right reasons.

I had a feeling she wouldn't be alone when she cried, later.

CHAPTER FOUR

I was a full-fledged member of the gang, minus one. The third part of the initiation was how I performed in a rumble. But for now, I was a Baron. I could swagger with the rest of them.

I didn't even have to learn the primer for gang kids; it was instinctive. Simple.

When he's down, kick for the head and groin.

Never make it on the scene unless you're shanked and the blade's got seven inches on a quick switch.

Avoid cops. Play it cool.

There aren't many rules in the primer for gang kids, but what few there are, all count. They're all easily understood because they use a simple, sound philosophy: it's a stinking life, so get your kicks while you can. The gang is home, the gang is mother and father and clergy and teacher; take what you want before some sonofabitch takes it first; tell them nothing—and don't get caught.

And today, in the five boroughs of New York City, and all across half-sleeping America, wherever the Hell of the cities forces kids into the gutters, young toughs are applying those rules.

When they're laughing at the authorities, they call themselves "the men," or "the guys" or simply "we are juvies." It's short for juvenile delinquent, but there's nothing short about the knives they carry, or the lengths they'll go to in obtaining revenge. They revel in the notoriety they receive in newspapers and cheap periodical exposés. Then they try to outdo the fabricated fantasies of writers who have never been down there in the gutter, on the turf with the kids; writers who are doing more damage with their wild yellow-journalism than they can imagine.

Get it straight right now: these aren't kids playing games of war; they mean business, bad business.

By now the kids are also aware of the potential dangers of the social worker and the honest reformer—they no longer trust them. When the gang counselor, youth worker, settlement attaché moves in, the rumbles cease, the kicks get less; oh, sure, there are less cats making it over from other turf on raids, and more policed dances, and the block cools off, but that only makes the scene that much more of a drag for them. So they tell the social workers what they want them to know, and keep the dark facts tucked into their boot tops.

Here are some of those dark facts.

The gang stud pays first homage to the club. He attends meetings religiously, he never finks on a brother member, he never crosses a member unless the circumstances are inevitable, and then, only under specified, almost formalized, conditions—equivalent to a duel. He is as ruthless as a Syndicate torpedo when those circumstances and conditions arise.

Armed combat in the world of the tenements is a make-shift thing. It is a field of endeavor that has allowed the old Yankee bathtub-inventor room to swing. While today a kid can mug a drunk and collect twenty-five dollars to buy himself a piece—a gun, that is—in New York it is still not the easiest thing to find a fence or a pawnbroker or a junk salesman or a gang pusher with that many pieces handy. So they invent their own weapons.

Forget the common utensils of destruction, the switchblade, the ironwood chair leg club, the broken bottle, the blackjack made from dumping two dozen half dollars into a U.S. Army cushion-sole sock, the brass knucks made in shop class by agile hands. Forget them for the moment, they can't be really classified as ingenious, nor can the lead pipes, the baling hooks or the sheath-knife carried behind the neck in an oiled case, so just discount them.

Consider for the moment such lethal weapons as the raw potato studded with double-edged razor blades. A perfect in-fighting tool used formerly by the Black Irish in their war with England, the kids have found it perfect for stripping the flesh from an opponent's face. And if the fuzz bust the rumble, why, you just roll the weapon down the most convenient sewer opening. Lost: only an old potato and a quarter's worth of Gillette blue blades.

Or how about that homemade cannon, the zip-gun, about which you've heard so much? Have you any idea how simple they are to make? Not the detailed and involved weapons made by kids who only want to sport a deadly-looking piece, but the quickly-made item to be used in a killing.

The tube-rod in a coffee percolator is the barrel. Did you know it's exactly right for a .22 calibre slug? Or perhaps it's not the stem from a coffee pot. Perhaps it's a snapped-off car radio antenna. Either one will do the job. They mount it on a block of wood for a grip, with friction tape, and then they rig a rubber-band-and-metal-firing-pin device that will drive the .22 bullet down that percolator stem or antenna shell, and kill another teen-ager. What they don't bother to tell you is that a zip-gun is the most inaccurate, poorly-designed, dangerous weapon of the streets. Not only dangerous to the victim, but equally dangerous to the assailant, for too often the zip will explode in the firer's hand, too often the inaccuracy of the homemade handgun will cause an innocent bystander to be shot. It is a booby trap of the most innocent-seeming sort, and there are many kids in Brooklyn (or in Queens, Long Island City and Astoria, where the Kicks, another club much given to the use of the zip, roam) with only two or three fingers on a hand, from having snapped that rubber band against the metal firing pin.

But there are even more terrifying weapons, if one only takes the time to seek them out:

Garrison belts, with the buckles honed to a razor's edge. Barracks boots with razor blades stuck between the toe and the sole, protruding just enough so that a fierce kick will slash the tendons of an opponent's legs, render him a cripple. The Molotov cocktail—gasoline and a rag packaged in a large size Coke or Canada Dry ginger ale bottle. Blinding fuse-packets of potassium nitrate and powdered magnesium, gauged to explode in a magnesium flash when they are thrown into someone's face.

The weapons of the gang kid have a charm all their own.

But more than that, gang warfare is typified by a callous disregard for Marquis of Queensbury rules, or for that matter, rules of simple decency. When they fight, they are amoral . . . totally without mercy . . . almost inhuman.

A cat that's down is a cat who can't bother you, man! Stomp him! Stomp him good! Put that lit cigarette in the bastard's eye! Wear Army barracks boots—kick him in the throat, in the face, kick him where he lives. Smash him from behind with a brick, cave in his effin' skull! Flat edge of the hand in the Adam's Apple! Use a lead pipe across the bridge of his nose—smash the nose and send bone splinters into the brain!

And after it's over, slip your switch or your piece to your Deb; let her shove it into her bra or garter belt, the waistband of her pants, to be carried boldly away from the rumble. The fuzz don't search the chicks, they get away clean. Or play it cool, use the spud-and-blades bit, and then heave the weapon down the nearest gutter.

No loss.

There's grocery and drug stores on every block.

The young rocks of the Barons (or the Blooded Royals, or the Kicks, or The Jolly Stompers, or The Egyptian Dragons, or The Centurions, pick one) think very much alike. Their morals and language, their dress and weapons, they're all much of a kind.

Imagination is a sometimes thing, but mimicry and the ability to pick up on something useful, to imitate what they have seen on television or in the movies, what they've learned from commando and judo manuals acquired through the mails, this is a talent well-developed in the gangs.

At one time the sincerest form of flattery was practiced so much, that each member of the Barons wore a black and gold basketball jacket, shiny satin, with the club name in bold script across the back, the wearer's name across the pocket. But the Barons, as with most kid gangs these days, finally realized advertising was poor form. The nice shiny satin jacket with BARONS scrawled big across the back was a signpost to every cop in the turf. They realized it was easier to keep a gang swinging if the fuzz didn't know they existed. So they made it mandatory that the jackets be hung away for good, and anonymity settled over the Barons, as far as ballyhoo was concerned, though the neighborhood knew who they were. It didn't need to be advertised in the *Amsterdam News*—the people knew.

The social structure of a juvenile gang is very much like that of a fraternity. There is a top man, a President, a cabinet of officers, and lay members. There may or may not be a girl's auxiliary—the Debs—and a sub-group of juveniles who are underage for the adult club, but are more or less "in training." These younger kids are usually used to run errands, case holdups, steal hub-caps and automobile parts for sale to swell the club treasury. They are Fagin's Tots, idolizing their older brothers and worshipping those members of the adult gang who have graduated from the streets to a life of crime, and inevitably, to prison.

It is the Twenties all over again, with the worship of hoodlumism returning. It is these snot-nosed youngsters who need to be saved.

Few gangs are interracial; it would appear the bigot and the narrow-minded are predominant in the gangs, but more likely it is the corrupting influence of parents with their casual dark references to "niggers" or "kikes" or "wops" or "spics" that does the trick. Were it not for the adult poisons poured into these kids' ears, the gang lines might easily cross color or race or religion. But since they hate Puerto Ricans and Negroes and Jews and Catholics, the gangs are generally made up (as was the Barons) of one nationality group or race, or cultural strain.

The female's position in the social structure of a street gang is cut and dried. She is property.

The chicks of gang kids are even more ruthless than their male counterparts, of that I'm certain. Their affairs with gang members are violent, often deadly, and if a girl is caught cheating, her punishment can range from a sound beating to the slicing of a pretty face so *no one* shows interest in her again. And they never talk. They never tell what happened. There are easier ways to commit suicide, more pleasant, quicker methods to take one's own life.

And when Debs fight, there are few sights as unbelievable. Perhaps ghastly is the proper word. It is a knockdown-blot-up of the first order, with such fury and horror it is impossible to describe without the use of a movie camera.

The knees, teeth, nails, and hair-pulling carried to a strange degree are merely openers. Knives, beer can openers, hatpins in the eyes, acid, pain pain pain! A girl jumped by more than one Deb can expect to have her face slashed for life, her body racked out of shape, her vitals explored with every foul, cutting implement sick and tormented minds can design.

The Debs join the club for kicks, and they'll get them, one way or another. Literally.

The current fad among kid gangs and their Deb auxiliaries is the carving of the current boy friend's initials in

63

the girl's back, arms, or more usually, breasts, with a knife.

A sign of undying affection.

At least until the next stud comes along; which makes it difficult for the chick with someone else's initials in her hide. I've seen Debs whose breasts looked like much-used trees bordering a Lover's Lane.

Names for Deb groups are usually imitative of the parent club (as in the case of The Baron Debs), but occasionally a bright youngster will name a girl's auxiliary The Rockettes, or The Ladies Aid, or The Bitches. It all depends on whether there is a member of more-than-average literacy and imagination, something rare in the gangs, where poverty and the fight for survival have combined to hold down the intelligence of most of the kids.

They aren't stupid, they just don't know any better.

With the antediluvian school system through which most of these kids are shunted, the out of touch with reality aspects of the Church, and the criminal negligence of parents, to what teachers do the gang kids resort?

CHAPTER FIVE

I was still a full-fledged member of the gang—minus
one. A rumble. I had to show how good I was in a fight.
But it seemed I might not make it that far. I had made
enemies in the gang: The slicers who had wanted a piece
of me in running the gantlet, friends of Flo who thought I
was a wise guy, a pair of generally surly types who liked
no one and were maintained on the club roster because
they were case-hardened fighters. I suspected I might have
to prove my worth long before the Barons hit another
rumble.

Of the immediate members of the gang—that is, regu-
lars, with whom I had the most contact—there were only
two of whom I was unsure. One was an unpleasant kid
with the unlikely name of Steigletz. They called him Candle, no explanation. He looked Spanish; great dark eyes
and black hair cut in an old-fashioned bowl-on-the-head
manner, all the more accentuating the *peon* look. He
despised Puerto Ricans, perhaps because he so resembled
them physically. He took every possible opportunity to an-
nounce his European heritage, and occasionally made
references to how cool the Nazis had been in gassing anyone who got in their way. It was a short hop, apparently,
from self-hatred because he faintly resembled what he
took to be a lesser ethnic group, to despising the entire

65

human race. He was a stocky boy, with broad, box-like shoulders, a deep chest and massive biceps. He kept himself in peak physical condition, another means of surmounting what he took to be a handicap, his appearance. Few kids in the gang would associate with him, much less actually chum it up. But Candle had one good friend, nonetheless.

Fat Barky was the son of a local character, Old Barky, who was renowned far and wide as the only man who would get down on all fours in a saloon and bark like a dog, in exchange for a shot of rye. His son, Fat Barky (almost 190 pounds), was forced to live with the knowledge that his father was a neighborhood joke. It made *him* a joke, too. Sublimation and compensation had turned Fat Barky into a bully, a loafer, a sadist, and—there were those who had reason to suggest—a pervert. He was not overly bright, and that, coupled with his doughy face, ham-like hands and massive, shapeless body made him a figure of some terror. He had been known to pick up and throw an antagonist thirty feet through a plate glass window, if the tremors struck him. He was an advocate of health foods, bar-bells and sunbaths on rooftops.

These two pretties disliked me for different reasons, but chiefly because Candle had wanted to slice me up a bit during the gantlet-run; I had thwarted him, and he felt cheated. In this particular boy, a feeling of having been cheated was equivalent to a slap in the mouth. He had allowed the mild distaste for me to grow within him as the days passed, until it was almost an obsession, brought on by the summer heat, the lack of excitement, and his mounting realization that he was getting too old to remain in the gang much longer, and might soon have to fend for himself in the adult world. It was an amalgam of reasons, and like the emotional volcano it created, it found release in hatred. Hatred of me. I was new in the gang, I was untested, I was a wise guy. Therefore, hate.

Fat Barky was his friend: his only friend, really. He didn't need much of a reason to hate. It was all built in.

So I had a pair of Kings aligned against me; God only knows how well I could have done making enemies if I had tried my fullest.

Yet in its ludicrousness, it was another lesson about the children of the gutters: they don't need logical reasons to hate. They are time bombs, set by a madman to go off at any time. Tap them, smile at them, walk past them and they explode. They are so filled with insecurities, hatreds, tensions, their fuses grow shorter and shorter. There is no logic, no sense at all to their animosities. If you are alive—you are a possible target for their fury.

It began, the chivvying, almost from the next day.

I had more or less taken on Filene as my chick, and in the eyes of the other Debs, that made me off-limits. There are occasional loose studs in the gang, but they hook up as quickly as possible with a steady (there is usually a good bit of nonsense about "love" and "playing house"—all tied up with the fraudulent standards of sex and affection shoved down these kids' throats by billboards, newspapers, television and the other guilty mass media). Reasons for tying the bonds as soon as possible are not only romantic, but economic and expedient. There aren't that many girls floating loose at any one time.

So I found it very strange when Flo made a pass at me in Ben's, the next day. Strange because we were not the best of friends, and strange because I was with Filene.

When Filene and I came through the door, I noticed a stillness in the mood of the place: an expectancy. Pooch and Fish were not there, and most of the kids I knew with any real familiarity were absent. But Fat Barky was lounging up against the juke box, slapping the red plastic of one side with a slab hand. I couldn't see into the booths in back, but there must have been Barons in them, because I heard voices. The stools up front were occupied by three girls—Cherry, Marcia and Flo whose feet were once again on the wall, as they had been the first time I made this scene.

Filene and I started to walk back, but Ben Adelstein's voice stopped us. "Hey, how about a new kind of shake?"

I turned to look at him, and for the first time in my life I knew when someone was trying desperately to tell me something with his face. Little Ben Adelstein was scared ... and not for himself.

I had my arm around Filene, and as Ben spoke again, I pulled her toward the counter with me. "Hey, kid, you want a new kind of shake I just invented?"

I answered him, but we both knew I wasn't asking about any milk shake. "What ya got for us, Ben?"

He drew us down the front of the counter, away from the stools, and said, very loud, "Never had a marshmallow milk shake, have you?" His eyes were flipping back toward the rear of the malt shop. He was trying to tell me there was something shaking back there; I tried observing over Filene's shoulder, searching the shadowy rear of the shop, but all I could see was Fat Barky, big as a house, leaning against that juke box.

I didn't dare ask right out what was the matter. The three girls were too near.

Then it all happened very fast, and I was in the middle of it. I started to say something nonsensical to Ben, and I felt a hand on my waist, and someone was shoving a large breast into my back. I half-turned, still holding Filene, and finding the movement difficult, and there was Flo, pressed up against me in the most awkward manner I could imagine.

She started saying some crap that was supposed to be a come-on; I wasn't even sure what it was—the girl had a way of speaking so that you didn't listen. It was like turning the volume all the way down on a television set and merely watching the comical movements of the speaker's lips. That was the way it was now.

"Hey, beat it, I'm with someone," I started to say.

She yelled. I mean she belted the place with a howl that would have lifted the scalp from a bald man. It was a sort of half-rape, half-hysterical shout, and before I knew what

68

was happening, one of those dim booths in the back had erupted and Candle was halfway down the line of stools, a fist pulled back, aimed at my mouth.

He was closely followed by the Heap, Fat Barky, who didn't even bother cocking a fist. Sheer momentum would have carried him right through me and out into the street.

I was still only partially aware of the dislike I'd engendered in these two, and for them to use the unhappy Flo as a foil, and try to bushwack me was something I could not quite conceive.

Until the moment Candle swung and took me flush in the mouth. I felt Filene being ripped away from me, a hot, sticky pain went all through the left side of my head, and I went straight down to the floor.

The next thing I saw was a boot sole, and it was rapidly descending on my face. I threw myself over and caught Candle's boot high on my shoulder. It hurt like the devil, and my arm went numb, matching my face. Everything was a misty, off-grey, and while I was still very much conscious, I had the feeling this beating was being administered to someone else, not me.

He kicked me in the backside, and I doubled over—dummying up—against the base of the counter, trying to keep my face and vitals protected by wrapping my arms and legs about myself, fetus-style. Candle kept right on dealing up belts to the can, and I was able to maneuver my body so he couldn't catch me in the kidneys.

In a few seconds—I *think* it was a few seconds—things began to clear for me and I could hear Filene screaming. She had tried to intercede and Flo had grabbed her by the hair. Now the two girls were struggling insanely against the wall, and Flo was getting the better of it, over Filene's small, slim body. And in one instant I tried to get up, felt more than saw Candle pulled back, heard Ben Adelstein yell, "That Candle started it!" and the kicking stopped at once. I moved around a trifle, looking up from under my arm, and there was Pooch and Fish and Connie and Mr.

Clean and half a dozen other Barons, two of them whip-arming Candle back against the magazine racks.

I tried to get up and found my legs wouldn't support me. One of them leaned down, and I got lifted bodily to my feet. Candle was in a half-nelson by Mustard, a kid with very blonde hair and not much sense. Candle's eyes were wild with the kill-light. He wouldn't have stopped till I was out of it completely, a broken back, a smashed rib cage, a punctured lung.

Pooch's face was storm dark.

"Okay, whatinahell's goin' on here? C'mon, what was it?"

Candle jumped in before I could collect my wits and figure out how my tongue was supposed to function. He began a tirade about how I was trying to horn in on every broad in the club, how I'd made unnecessary advances on Flo, while in the company of Filene, how I was a bad influence in the gang, and a wise sonofabitch and how I'd cheated everyone in the gantlet, and how he didn't even think I'd carried through on the second part of the initiation and it was either Candle or me, and that was all there was to it.

I've never seen a kid so young, get so red in the face, in so short a time. He was livid. Pooch was thoughtful. I was still semi-conscious.

Filene piped in, "That isn't so! It didn't happen like that! *He* started it, him and that stinking creep, Flo!"

Pooch motioned her to silence, and I knew he had to make a Prez-like decision. He had to maintain some status in the eyes of his gang, and at the same time he had to solve the problem without putting down one or another of us. It was a Solomon-level problem, but Pooch solved it admirably. As far as he was concerned.

"Okay. I don't want no more fighting in here, and I want some peace between you two guys. If it's got to be one or the other, it'll have to be settled in a stand. That okay with both of you?"

"Yeah, great!" chirped Candle.

I didn't say anything for a second. A stand ... a knife fight with Candle ... was I up to it? Here was a tough who had been handling a switchblade since he was old enough to tell one from a can opener. I wasn't at all sure I could stand up to him. And if I didn't, there would be no question about what would happen to me. I'd be found in an alley sliced methodically. I might not die, but the difference was too slight to worry about.

But I had no choice.

"Okay. Okay, by me. Name the place, and the weapons."

It was a little like a Heidelberg duel. Pooch called for seconds, and Candle named Fat Barky immediately. I looked around and settled on Fish. They went off into a booth in back with Pooch, and talked in low murmurs for fifteen minutes.

Filene used a wet napkin on my face. I tried smiling at her, but it hurt, so I grimaced. Candle slouched against the counter, surrounded by Barons who wanted to keep us apart, and he smoked one after another.

Finally, Pooch, Fish and Fat Barky came back. "It'll be Saturday morning, the dumps. Switches, Comanche style."

I almost keeled over. Comanche-style. A regulation size hankie twisted to its full length, clenched in our teeth, one hand tied behind each of our backs, and the knife in the free hand. We had only the distance of the hankie separating us. It was the most deadly, the least-quarter-given style of gang-fighting known. Pooch was determined to settle it once and for all. The chill in my neck and shoulders spread.

That next Saturday Fish came for me in a 1952 Ford he had either borrowed or heisted, and with two other Barons in the back seat, we motored over to the garbage dump.

It was a great brown-black expanse, on the edge of the waterfront, with great piles of burning refuse dotting the horizon like blank anthills on fire. It stank. I was scared out of my mind. This was no game and it was certainly not research; this was for real, and I regretted the whole thing.

I must have tried to pull out of Brooklyn, disappear into Manhattan, a hundred times between Pooch's announcement and that morning. Why I'd stayed was more inertia than guts.

The Ford came through a break in the hurricane fence surrounding the far end of the dumps, and Fish poured it to the floor, speeding till the group finally came into sight. There were perhaps half a dozen cars, pulled into a circle, noses inward, and all the Barons, their Debs, the junior toughs from the secondary club (The Boppers, or the Baron Juniors) were all standing around, blowing pot or just talking.

Fish floored it and raced up to the group at sixty-five, at the last moment standing full on the brakes and pulling a two-wheel drift that shot a spray of dirt in a wide arc.

The engine stalled and we got out of the car.

Candle looked as big as a mountain.

Pooch was there with his drag, a girl alternately called Goofball and Mary. She was a hippy broad, with big blue eyes and blonde hair from a bottle she should never have uncorked. It was her face that drew me. There was a look in it that I had never before seen, and have glimpsed only once since that time:

On the face of a woman staring up at a guy on a window ledge. She wanted him to take the dive.

Goofball wanted someone to die.

This, then, was the expression on the faces of the titled ladies of the Roman court in attendance at the Circuses. It was a chilly, indrawn-breath look that said volumes. Volumes from Dachau and Auschwitz and the Colosseum and every temple of horrors from the first cave to Torquemada's Inquisition Chambers. Such depravity, such absolute absence of humanity, was the thing I first saw upon leaving Fish's car. It was the worst possible effect. Any fun and games I might have thought to pull off, were forgotten in the sight and planes and lights of that girl's face.

72

She clutched Pooch's arm, and pressed her breast against it, oversexed with the possibility of blood and dismemberment. I swore I would not satisfy her filthy appetite that morning.

And still, Candle looked as big as a mountain.

"G'morning," I said, jauntily.

It went over like a leper in an elevator. And Candle Steigletz snickered like a seven-year-old. He was wearing a heavy sweater and a shirt under his leather jacket, and I was abruptly glad I had worn my own sweater under my black leather jacket. Protection across the belly and on the arms was a precious thing.

He looked like a bit-player in an Orozco painting. The black bangs hanging down almost to his thick eyebrows, the baleful black eyes sheltered under brows that hid the light and direction of his glance. That, too, was something disturbing:

Point: when you knife-fight, watch the knife hand, of course, but more important, watch the other guy's eyes. It tells before his hand when he's going to swing steel. A squint means a strike.

"You ready, Cheech?" Pooch asked. Goofball wet her lips. Oh, how I wanted to squash that broad!

"I'm ready," I said. I was ready to run, *that's* what I was ready to do.

"You ready, Candle?" Pooch turned to my opponent.

For the answer he gave a funny little wiggle to his arm and the switch-blade dropped down his sleeve, into his hand. He brought it up carefully and pressed the stud on the side. The blade leaped up into sight, and the early morning grey was caught all along the six inch length of the honed blade.

I dipped my body and came up from the boot with my own Italian stiletto. It wasn't a switch, and this was the first time the gang had had occasion to see how I uncorked it.

In all fairness, it is a more impressive unveiling than merely pressing a button. I whipped my arm sidewise,

73

catching my thumb-nail under the slightly protruding tip of the blade, and flipped it out as my arm came around in a great snake-like sweep.

The blade, the hand, the arm quivered to a halt in firing position. I saw a momentary look of uncertainty cross Candle's broad, flat face. There were murmurs from the crowd. A real grandstand play; I only hoped I was able to continue my performance.

Filene was there, behind a group of Debs, and I heard her thin voice say something reassuring.

"Okay," said Pooch, "here's the handkerchief." He drew a fresh, clean, white handkerchief out of his side pocket and opened it up full. He took alternate corners in each hand and twirled it the way kids do a towel in the locker room of a gym, when they're going to snap each other's bare backsides. Then, when it was a two-foot strip, he dropped it on the dirty ground between us.

I moved slowly but surely to it and picked it up.

I shook it out a bit, pulling down its length so it would stay long and tight, and put one end in my mouth, wadding it tightly behind my clenched teeth so it could not slip out. I extended the opposite end to Candle, delicately, watching his eyes all the while. They were brightly on me, as he took it.

CHAPTER SIX

Candle took the hankie in his mouth and maneuvered it with tongue and teeth until the cloth was settled properly. A faint trickle of spittle edged from the corner of his mouth.

We were now separated across a two foot restraining line of taut cloth. We moved toward each other and the hankie drooped in the middle. Pooch stepped behind Candle and Fish moved around back of me. I watched as Pooch unbuckled Candle's wide garrison belt, and pushed it back through two loops till it was loose enough to serve the purpose: he took Candle's left arm and put it behind his back, inserting it between Candle's belt and pants. Then he moved to the front, pulled the belt tight and buckled it, two notches shorter than before. Fish did the same to me. We were amputated now, one-armed knife-fighters, with the difference that my left arm, my knife-arm, was free, and Candle was on the right side free. It was a very slight advantage for me, coming in on the off-side.

It was the first time I had ever really been grateful at being left-handed.

Pooch stepped in close and put hands around the backs of our necks; he pulled our heads close together, and I got a full view, as close as I ever wanted, of Candle's *peon* face. It was an unhappy face, fronting an unhappy kid.

I didn't want to fight him.

"Now you know the rules of a stand?" Pooch asked. He didn't give us time to answer, but went directly on: "Nobody swings till Mary gives the go-ahead—" he motioned to Goofball, who stood with moist, expectant lips, "—and then you use anything you want, so long as one hand stays behind alla time, and you don't drop the kerchief. One of ya drops the kerchief, he loses, the other guy's got rights to the loser. A fall is a fall and that's it. The fallen guy is the loser. Winner, any which way, he's got full rights. All the way."

In short, the loser was dead.

Pooch moved back, and instantly we pulled the hankie two feet tight, our backs arched, bodies curved to put us as far away at swinging level as possible. The arm-swinging range was exactly two feet ... with the other guy's knife in the line of fire. A kid with gorilla arms hanging below his knees would have been a shoo-in. We moved idly, maneuvering. The wind blew in off the river. My eyes started to unfocus, and I blinked them three or four times quickly, to put me back where I belonged.

Now was no time to crap out.

I planted my feet apart and waited for Goofball to give us the word. Candle's eyes were totally in darkness now; I could only see the flat planes of his cheeks that telegraphed nothing. Out of the corner of my eye I could see Pooch putting his arm around Goofball's shoulders, whispering something to her, and she tittered idiotically.

Then she drew in breath to yell and I knew the balloon was about to go up. She screamed right at us:

"Go GO!"

Candle jerked back sharply on the hankie and it started to slip from between my teeth. I'd lose by default. The cheap cloth gave an ominous tearing sound and I swung my knife in wide, flat arcs, moving forward and teeth-winding the hankie so I had it more firmly between my jaws.

I almost wound too much, almost came too close. Candle made a first tentative slash at me, trying to break through the windmill attack I was laying down to cover my teeth-winding of the hankie, and he almost made it. I was almost too close, with too little hankie between us. I stopped winding, wadded it behind my clenched teeth and settled down to fight.

Then we were equally apart, the hankie tight, the knives enough of an extension to gut, if the opening came.

We circled; stepping, stepping, stepping carefully, measuring each movement. Footwork had to be close, and a misstep could send a guy down, his feet fouled, his windpipe exposed. And down meant out.

Pretty quick the ground was worn into a dark brown rough circle as we went tail-around-head past each other. The Barons and their Debs fanned out, watching, making sure that a wild swing could not touch them. We bent forward from the shoulders, putting our bellies as far back as possible.

We stopped every half-circle, our feet wide apart, swinging for an opening, fencing for a thrust, making certain we didn't throw ourselves off-balance.

I could hear Candle grunting, and my own explosions of sweat only made me more aware of how tired my arm was getting already—and nothing had happened.

Strange thoughts beat at my mind, and I had the feeling this was a play or some histrionic charade. It had to end; and then Candle's arm would come up from below, and I'd counter with my own sleeve and the force of his swing would bounce off me, deadening my forearm, and I'd know it was no sham. This was the goods. I swung back in defense. He had me backing off now, as much as I was able to back off with that frigging hankie between my teeth, tethering me. I was starting to stoop over, and I knew it was a dead giveaway to the *peon* that I was weakening. He came on that much harder, and I found myself bouncing roundhouse slashes off my jacketed arm.

One got through, I heard the leather rip heavily, and

he'd brought across the first successful swing of the game. The sonofabitch moved in for an early kill.

He brought it up from around his thigh, arcing over in a full overhead jab. It came down like a swooping hawk and I ducked aside, kicking him in the ass as he went past. It threw him completely off-balance, and as he went skinning past me, the hankie snapped tight, nearly jerking him off his feet. He spun as best he could and wiggled the blade awkwardly in defense, trying to keep me away till he could get his feet under him.

I didn't give him a break. I juggled back, dragging him with me, but I moved too fast and almost fell over myself.

In a moment we were both stable, both wary again, circling each other as before. I still had a slight edge because I was a southpaw, but it didn't make up for his greater reach, and the fact that I was getting tired. I had a hunch he worked out with weights, the bastard.

He parried and countered each thrust and riposte I tried to eel past him, and I did the same for his sloppy attacks. But we weren't getting anywhere, and pretty quick one of us was going to goof and that was it.

He called me a dirty name for vagina, through his clenched teeth, and I brought across a zig-zag slash from right to left that caught him with his guard lowered. I cut him on the chin—the blood came out in a thin, crooked line from his jawbone to his lower lip, and he squealed wildly. I felt a sudden exuberance; so this was what it was like to kill a man!

It was worth doing, suddenly, and I knew how people could get carried away. It was plunging down a steep snowy hill on a sled, like whipping around a turn on a carnival ride, like flooring a car . . . it was strange and weird and wonderful—and then he cut me back.

His knife sliced right through my jacket, my sweater, my shirt and my T-shirt, and entered my body, and all the fun and glamour and buoyancy were gone. It was pain. Terrible pain. Worse than falling down and cutting my face, and worse than being hurt for a reason. This was

78

stupid, and it was death I was fooling with, not gamesmanship! This was no movie or TV act where we'd shake hands and walk away afterward. It was the McCoy, the goods, the real stuff, and I was scared again, worse than before.

And still I fought on. Because I couldn't do anything else.

My hair broke loose from its careful, rigid pompadour, and flopped over my eyes. I couldn't waste my knife-hand to swipe it away, though. I couldn't blow it back away with my lips, so I tossed my head quickly, right at the top of a full-arm swing.

It fell back and I resigned myself to my handicap. Candle's hair was flat, gave him no trouble, but what he had considered an advantage—the heavy leather jacket—was not. Unlike mine, it was almost skin-tight, and the jacket bunched against the insides of his elbows, made swinging difficult, and sometimes cut short his reach.

Then we went into an interminably long period of short, dagger-like thrusts and kicking. Around and around we went, and I don't know how long it was, just the sound of my grunts and straining, the sounds of his exertions and sweat coming off the both of us. None of the others spoke. It was too much fun to watch.

Candle kicked out with a faking movement and I leaped back, jerking Candle's neck at the end of the hankie. But he fooled me . . . he came on instead of pulling back to right himself, and his arm went around my neck, and that knife was in back of me somewhere. My own arm was wedged in between us, the knife harmlessly hanging down between our legs. I fought in close to him, trying to break his stranglehold, and we nudged each other roughly with our shoulders, edging each other a few inches, then back again.

I was starting to grey-out. He had my windpipe, somehow, and I knew another few moments would finish me. I lunged forward, carrying him with me, and banged my head down in a sharp, vicious bird-like peck. My forehead

79

caught him squarely across his nose, and he fell back in pain, almost screaming, allowing the hankie to sag in the middle. I drew back to the end of the tether, and gasped hugely through my nose, trying to get the clouds and scum and cobwebs off my brain. Finally, I steadied myself for the swing I knew had to come. He thought he had me on the ropes—and he wasn't far wrong—and he was going to put it all into one monstrous attempt. But the attack came from an entirely new direction. His knife hand stayed plainly in sight, and he kicked me square in the crotch.

I felt the blood draining out of my face, and the pain came up like a screwdriver inserted in my privates. It was so bad I couldn't make a sound. All air went out of me and I started to fall backward. He hit me again, with the balled fist and the handle of his knife, right across the left temple. Someone cracked my skull like an empty paper bag. I started to fall, and I grabbed out, and he came across with the knife again, going for my throat, and I threw up my hand, and I felt the razored edge of the blade slice across my palm. Blood spurted all over everything. Oh, *Jeezus!*

I wanted to scream, but something made me hold that hankie between my teeth, no matter what, and I sank to my knees, wadding the cloth tighter as blood poured across my hand and down my arm.

Candle stepped back for the death-swing and nothing, not a damned thing, passed before my eyes, except the steel that was about to be imbedded in my chest. It came up like a jet from around the *peon's* knees as he bent to drive it further into me, and I jerked sidewise, throwing out one leg like a Russian Cossack dancer. Candle went on past me, over the leg, and down in a sprawling heap, ass over teakettle, and the hankie popped from his mouth with a soft snap.

I was on my feet in an instant, and as he tried to get to his feet I kicked him squarely in the mouth. He went back down, bits of him all over the place. But he wasn't finished. He tried it again, and this time I took him under the chin with the toe of my boot. His eyes rolled up in his head and he gagged and puked and fell right back over, the knife still clenched in his fist.

I looked down at him lying there, ruined, and the hankie hanging idiotically from my mouth.

The Barons went nuts. "Kill him! Jam him! Jam him! Knife the bastard, knife him, man, knife him!" they screamed, and everything whirled and spun and my flesh ached, and my groin was on fire, and the blood, oh Christ, the blood was all over my hands, and all over him, and everything . . .

A foot came out of the crowd and jammed down on Candle's hand with the knife, and then kicked the blade out of his reach. He was unconscious, completely out of it.

"Get him, he was gonna put you down!" Goofball yelled, right in my ear.

I stared down at him, lying there on his back, and for a second it all went away. The wind blew at me, and I heard the water, and freedom, and pity, and surliness and madness, and then it all went away again. My knees turned to peanut butter, my hands went limp, and I saw the sky as I went over backward, all grey-white and speckled with large dots of red and black and green and blue and then the black got bigger, and so help me God, I passed out with my feet almost touching Candle's feet.

I went far away, very fast.

It didn't last nearly as long as I wanted it to last. Very soon the black started to widen and draw down, like a big piece of black rubber, being stretched tight. Then it spread and grew thin in spots, and I saw grey, then white, behind it. Then the grey became an overall shade, and the painful spears and rents of white burst upon me fully.

It was Filene's face I saw, first thing. She had a look of absolute horror in her eyes, and at that moment I realized they were as brown as a candy bar. Her long, straight hair was hanging over her shoulders, and she had my head in her lap. It was straight out of *McCall's*, and I didn't mind a bit. I tried to raise myself, and everything blew out like an overloaded fuse. I went down again.

It was a long time before I came back again, and when I did, my skin felt open at every pore. Someone—Filene and Fish, I learned later—had bound up the thin cut on my left forearm and the deeper gash in my palm. I was blood all over and my head ached from the garrotting I'd taken. There's no use talking about the pain between my legs where he'd kneed me; it was unbelievable.

They had Candle propped up against someone's car wheel, and he was in very bad shape. It had not been too far away from total destruction; insanity had held me for a moment, and I saw how far one human being could go against another, if the reins were loosened. It made me very ill.

Pooch came swaggering over, as though I was a brother returned from the wars, and he threw an arm over me as Fish and a boy whose name I did not know lifted me to my feet. "Well, he's all yours," he said, waving a salutary hand at the fallen Candle.

Then he handed me Candle's blade. It was a big switch with green plastic side panels, made of Solingen steel and sharper than mine had been, even after my honing it for hours. That was it; Candle was mine. He was my bait; I was the victor, and if I wanted to open his jugular, they'd stand and watch (and Goofball would clap her hands in childish glee, no doubt). I could do as I pleased with his life. The law of the jungle was nakedly employed.

Candle stared up at me as I tottered over to him, aided by Fish on my right arm. His eyes were turned up into the morning light, and I could see both an open fear and an omnipresent challenge. His lips were parted slightly, in an infinitely callous expression. He didn't want to die, but he wasn't going to crawl. Perhaps he wasn't emotionally capable of crawling.

I looked down at him for a long second, and his sneer

grew like a flower opening to the sun. It spread across his *peon* face, and I found it difficult to combat it. For the first time in my life I literally held another person's life in my hands. I could kill or not, as I chose.

It was a heady feeling. There is no way to explain it; an Army infantryman, lying doggo in a ditch with his M-1 sights dead on an enemy, waiting to slowly squeeze off a round, knows what I mean. A housewife in Yonkers or Silver Spring, Maryland, can never know. It is unlike any other aphrodisiac or narcotic in the world. I had a knife, I had free passage, and I was master of not only my own Fate, but this gutter kid's, as well.

"I ought to put this right into you," I said. It was a wasted effort. He knew the moment I spoke that I was going to let him live. *He* knew it, and the gang knew it. And their respect for me dropped a notch. I was a hard-case, there was no doubt of that; even though I was a short bastard the fight had proved I could handle myself; but I wouldn't send that blade into Candle's body, so I wasn't a mean stud. I would never be able to take up residence in Death Row; they would never look on me as a cold number.

"Big man," Candle jibed at me.

I stooped down and grabbed him by his hair, pulled him halfway up. "You ever come near me again, *mienda*, I'll open you up right." Then I threw him back down roughly, laid the blade under my boot, and bent up sharply.

The blade snapped.

I threw down the broken knife, at his feet. He was a crushed warrior; his lance had been shattered; he was out of the lists, and I was the new champ of the hardcases.

Filene's eyes were moist and compelling.

I wanted to sleep for a week.

So this was authenticity. Gathering material in the field. I felt a leaden awareness in me, that I had been fooling myself, trying to glamorize the job.

This was a rotten way to go ... sliced open like a dead

fish, left to die in a garbage dump. I swore I'd never fight like that again. Ever. Even if they killed me.

I had no idea I would be tested again so soon, and that I'd have to defend myself again, come closer to death or dealing death, again. But it *was* to come, too soon.

CHAPTER SEVEN

Remembering ten weeks in a certain time-sequence is often difficult. A great deal can happen in ten weeks. A life can change or begin or end in ten weeks. But remembering ten weeks running with the children of the streets is not too difficult at all, for most of the time is spent waiting. The devil of the kids, the boredom known as Nothing's Shaking, possesses easily. The lounging in T-shirt and jeans before the malt shop, the standing on corners, swinging around and around on the lamp post, the sitting on stoops honing the knife . . . all the hours and days wasted, wasted, just waiting. "I'm just waitin' till I'm old enough to join up inna Merch' Marine like my big bruddah Sid." That's the story, right there. Waiting. Waiting and watching, and helping things along if it gets too peaceful. The absolute boredom of summer hot streets, sticky armpits, dry mouths, cigarette after cigarette tasting like cornsilk. The waiting and watching, till even the prospect of balling a piece of jailbait loses sparkle. That is the commonest denominator for the kids. They wait.

That was how it went for several weeks after my stand with Candle. The *peon* kept out of my way, and there were rumors of tossing him out of the gang, just on general principles. His friends ceased to be his friends, and the mark of the man on his way out was put on him when Ben Adelstein cut off his credit.

Then the rumble noises began to spread all through lower Brooklyn.

A war was in the brewing between the Barons and the toughest, largest gang in the city at that time. The Puerto Rican Flyers. A club rumored to have half a dozen submachine guns someone's brother had liberated from the US Army. A club that drank blood, it was said. A club whose members knew a code of honor that meant they got a full on-bended-knees apology for the slightest affront, or it was a stand to the finish. The rottenest club in town, it was said.

And the rumors of rumble spread.

It had started at a YMCA dance on a Friday night. A Flyer scout had found out about the Y dance in Baron territory, and for a week the Manhattan gang had planned to crash the spin. They made the scene late in the evening, when the dancers had already begun to stick close and many couples had disappeared into the parking lot. There was pot circulating, and a few bottles, and everyone was just about hammered enough to forget where they were.

A nameless Flyer stud took over a Baron girl—not a Deb, merely a date—while her boy friend was out corking up on Sneaky Pete.

The other girls, most of them Debs, made a short haul to the Baron who had left the scene, and gave him the word.

When he got back, the Flyer was belly-up to his girl, and a stand was called on the spot. Cooler heads prevailed, and the stand was moved out into the parking lot.

All the Barons and Flyers filed quietly out to the parking lot to build a wary circle as their two gladiators went at it. The Flyer was shanked, but the Baron had anticipated no trouble, and had to borrow a weapon from a friend. It wasn't a study in grace or ethics, but it looked as though matters might settle with one of the participants getting nicked, until a hopped-up Flyer with a big taste for action decided things were waltzing, and pulled a zip. He put a .22 slug through the chest of the Baron in the stand, and things broke out heavy.

I was not there, but one of the guys relayed the story, in that surrealistic "I-was-at-a-movie-and-it-went-like-this" manner employed by kids with very little imagination. The way he told it, the United Nations would have forgotten various Asiatic tension zones to handle the case. But from diffuse and diverse reports I was able to define what had happened, fairly closely.

Three Barons had jumped the kid with the zip and stomped his head into the gravel of the parking lot. No other clear duels were contracted, because in a matter of seconds the lot was a swarm of milling, jamming, swearing and fighting guys and Debs.

The Flyers came off the worse for wear. They were out-numbered three-to-one, as the Barons were aided by non-committed warriors from friendly gangs, or just plain neighborhood kids who knew which side their turf was buttered on.

No one died (death is a seldom thing, though crippling and scarring are not), and the Flyers escaped in a stolen car. The Barons gave chase, but turned off once in Manhattan, for they were nearing Flyer turf.

But the next day, the Barons got their revenge.

Ten of them invaded Flyer turf and caught a lone stud, walking on his block. They jumped him from a slow-moving car and threw him through the front window of a nearby bar and grill. The boy went to the hospital with facial lacerations and his esophagus open. I don't know whether he lived or not; I never heard a later medical bulletin.

It went quiet the rest of Saturday, and Sunday as well.

On Monday, the Flyers busted the trade high school where most of the Barons put in token appearances from time to time, and caught one of the original Friday night gladiators in his shop class. Ten of them held off the class and the shop instructor with a sawed-off shotgun and a

Luger pistol (as well as assorted sharp edges) while three of their buddies worked over the offending Baron with keyhole saws and ball peen hammers.

The boys left him hanging by his collar from one of the posts of a wood lathe, and completely vanished. The Baron joined the Flyer of Saturday forenoon among the lists of those needing medical attention. Both arms had been broken, as well as his nose, both cheekbones, his collarbone and left leg. He had a multiple concussion, and five shattered ribs. He was lucky he'd been left alive: one of the tormenters had used a keyhole saw on his face.

The War Counselors got together at the 42nd Street Nedick's at that point.

I was called in on Tuesday, for my opinion of the arrangements. Somehow it had gotten out that I read books; I was thus considered a "very hip guy" and my opinion was suddenly sought on such esoteric matters as:

What battleground will be used? What time? What kind and limit of weapons? Would Debs be employed? What was the rumble on the fuzz in that area, and this area, and the other area over there, huh?

A methodical procedure that would have done credit to a Disraeli. Machinations straight out of Machiavelli's "The Prince."

And while I was not an official War Counselor (at that point), I was able to introduce a few tactics that startled and pleased the young warriors. Oh, I was a very large cat that week.

Finally, the bickering ended, the demands settled and the lines drawn, the studs began sharpening their knives. This was to be a big rumble, a war in full dress, and this time the settlement workers would get no advance info on the scene, nobody was going to talk them out of it ... this was the topic of conversation, the building of prestige, the whole show, all wrapped and waiting for the main players to step in.

We had several secret weapons. One of them was a kid

named Fenster (nicknamed Fence) who had somehow (I was never sure how) acquired a Navy Very pistol that shot flares; another was a Spanish-American chick who had been double-balling (sleeping around in both turfs) a Baron and a Flyer, who could be at least fifty percent counted on to spill the other team's secrets and plans; a third was a carload of rifles the gang had stolen on Thursday. I had been involved in that ploy, rather intimately.

(I must make it clear at this point that not everything I did while as a member of the Barons was legal; I make no apologies for this. It can be chalked up to "method acting" or protective coloration or milking my material for everything in it—whichever seems to exonerate me most fully. And you may ask yourself what I asked *myself* so many times numbers lack meaning: how far do you go? Where do you say no further? When they knock down an old Polish lady with two full shopping bags of groceries, for chuckles, do you join in, or hold back? When they say use the knife or you're out of it, do you play the attentive hero with morality, or do you snap the blade into firing position? I can't make answers for anyone else; I can only say for myself, and in my own defense, if such seems needed, that I wanted to wring every drop of juice from the rotting vegetable that was a gang kid's life, and to do it, I had to *be* a gang kid. Not just intellectually, but emotionally. Down to the last nerve end, the last mood, the final indelicacy and indecency. It has to be tasted in its vilest potions to have validity. Halfways, niceties, all these merely intrude. So I am not asking for approbation, merely understanding. And a firm grasp on the concept of acts that are acts for themselves alone.)

With thirty bucks these days (garnered from selling stolen hub-caps or peddling pilfered appliances from shops or apartments), any kid can own a gun. He calls it a piece. He buys it from unscrupulous hock-shop shylocks or liaison men for fence groups. A piece is more effective than a zip. If you want to kill a guy, don't play around with the idea; get a piece and blow his screwing head off.

The only trouble was that there weren't enough $30 Barons around. Money was tight and so the middle-men would have to be eliminated. The gang (after Pooch's decision) moved to ignore the slimy little pawnbrokers.

The Barons were clever enough not to stage a robbery in their own territory. Good relations—up to a point—are necessary to the continuing existence of any club, and riots, robberies, rapes in home turf can only go on so long before the neighbors start to bang the ceiling with a broom handle. Then the shopkeepers and merchants recognize that they have a crime wave on their hands, and begin to point out the kids on the streets to the fuzz.

So the Barons rode the IRT, the BMT, the Independent Subway, calmly, coolly, looking like studs out for an evening of obnoxious fun . . . and they made their heists in rival gang turf.

The neighborhood chosen for my group was in lower Manhattan. We made it in Fish's heap, and the mark was a sporting goods shop singled out by Baron scouts.

The job was handled with such professional expeditiousness, I was shocked into admiration. Calm, collected, planned, very much like a military maneuver, tactically accurate and slotted to the second.

It was professional in timing and execution, as though they had been born to it. Where do they learn such things? TV, movies, true detective magazines, older brothers with enviable records from Dannemorra to big Q, Joliet to Alcatraz. Where there is a need for education, and a desire, primers are easy to come by.

Three kids handled the entry. One of them used a roll of adhesive tape, unrolling a taped circle on the plate glass of a door. While he did it, two others found the burglar alarm and jet-sprayed five cans of shaving cream into its mechanism so its bell would not be heard when the door was opened. It was a trick I'd seen used in a French motion picture. The first boy, in the meanwhile, was busy with a glass-cutter. A quick flathand smash while holding tightly to the tape (a *handle* of tape is attached under the

circle-tape beforehand) and a round of glass hangs inside
the shop. A fast reach inside, unbolt the door and open it,
grab the glass with the free hand, and everyone is inside,
without noise, without sweat.

The alarm rang, and it rang hard. But it didn't ring
very loud. Not with five cans of shaving cream sprayed
into its guts. We cleaned the place, and came away with a
trunkload of hunting rifles, three revolvers that had been
in the rear of the shop being repaired, and perhaps fifty
boxes of ammunition, most of them the wrong calibers for
the weapons we'd stolen.

There were other raids, though, and when the final ar-
mament was stacked in the club room, we had usable
tools to the tune of twenty-six rifles (from standard .30-
.30's to a lovely Husqvarna Swedish .30-.06 heavy hunting
rifle), five revolvers, three pistols—and the Very pistol.
That fails to include all the home-made zip guns, battering
rams, blunt instruments and sharp instruments. It would
have been a handy stack of force for any rebel group
from Cuba to Laos.

And in their own way, I suppose, these, too, were reb-
els.

Strictly without cause.

The upcoming Monday night was to be JD-Day. The
fight was to begin at eleven o'clock in the section of Prospect Park known as "The Jungle" (in the general vicinity
of Grand Army Plaza). Pickets and scouts could be laid
out earlier, but the full force of the operation was to begin at eleven o'clock, no sooner. Intelligence reports had
indicated the neighborhood beat cops were no problem for
almost an hour, though that figure could be cut to ten
minutes if any of the apartment-dwellers living on the
Avenues bordering the Park heard the sounds of combat.
But there was the chance that the woods and traffic would
sop up the noise initially. From fifteen minutes to half an
hour was the estimated fighting time . . .

The more I think about it now, the more I realize these

kids actually believed they were fighting for justice or some other equally abstract concept. They did not think of themselves as rotten kids rumbling. This was a matter of honor, and they were the Good Guys, ten gallon hats and white horses. The lousy spic Flyers were the Bad Guys—just as black as evil itself.

I tried talking to them during the week preceding the rumble. I have only one regret: that I was unable to tape their voices, for the conversations from memory lack much of the weariness and hopelessness of their discussions. The sense that there is really no future for them, the ineffectual animosity of their foul language; it all seems hollow without the harsh voices to lend reality.

The first one I talked to was Pooch. I got him to come out for a cup of coffee, and sat opposite him in a one-arm joint, trying to be two people at the same time.

"How long you been Prez?" I asked.

"About two years, almost two years, why?" he came back at me, instinctively wary at someone prying into his background or that secret room where the boy himself lived.

"Just wonderin', that's all."

"Well, I been Prez for almost two years."

"Uh-huh."

"Why'd you ask that? You know somethin' I don't know?"

I moved in, logically I hoped. "No, I was just thinkin', *you* know, maybe one of us'd get put down for good Monday, and what've we got to show for it?"

He looked at me quizzically. "What the hell you talkin' 'bout?"

I tried to explain, keeping to the semi-inarticulate patois and hand-movements of the street kids. "Well, dig; I mean, here you been Prez for two years—almost—and what if you pick up a bash Monday night? What's the club gonna do? They'll find some other guy and forget you. So what you got to show for all the sweat and the bopping?"

He bit the inside of his cheek. He was thinking. It was

painful to watch him try formulating an abstract concept. "Well, I mean, that'd be that, wouldn't it?" That was the closest he could come.

In that moment, no matter how many stinking things that boy had done, I felt great pity for him. He was, literally, voiceless in the world. He sat there, thinking himself strong and impregnable, and he was the weakest, most vulnerable kid I'd ever seen. He couldn't get a handle on life. He knew there were things he was missing, ways of living that he was denying, but he'd been on the treadmill so long he was unable to get off. I felt empathy for him, and sympathy, but most of all pity. And anger, too. Anger for all the parents and teachers and clergymen and social workers who had missed the boat with this kid, who were now content to merely hate him and track him through the smelly city streets, and prattle about *juvenile delinquency,* without realizing what it really was, without the simple understanding that it is the voicing of protest against a world that has no place for them.

"Yeah, sure," I answered simply, "but I mean what would you do with yourself if you wasn't in the club? I mean, like what would you be if you could be anyone?"

He stared at his coffee and then at his hands, and then at me. He'd probably never had a conversation like this before, and he was uneasy. Yet he could not simply call me a fink and get up from the table. We'd come farther than that. I had been speaking to *him,* not to the phony image he had been casting to everyone.

"Listen," he finally burst out, "I don't give a damn for none of that. You can't make it unless you got bread, lots of bread, and I know damned well I ain't gonna have none of it unless I work in some effing factory and I'd sooner shit than go into one of them. I'm just waitin' for one thing, man . . . I'm just waitin' till I get old enough, then I'm gonna enlist in the Merch' Marine."

He downed his coffee in a gulp, tossed a couple of coins on the table, and left the joint and me, sitting staring at the empty seat. Just as empty as his life.

CHAPTER EIGHT

Time was growing short before the rumble. And in that reckless, caged-animal attitude of the young hood, the Barons found their furies constrained. They went looking for trouble to whet their appetites, to let them try their muscles, to show them how tough they were.

They found their scapegoat.

A lone Negro boy playing basketball in a schoolyard.

Few gangs are interracial, except as I've mentioned before. It would appear that the lousy job of bring-up done on these kids has also imbued them with the narrow-minded, bigoted ideas of their elders. They hate Negroes. They also hate Puerto Ricans, Jews, Russians, anyone who differs from their particular accepted religious and racial norm in the turf. They tied the boy to one of the basketball standards, and worked him over. Six of them worked him over.

I wasn't there, but when I heard the story, told with mass braggadocio, with much laughter, my blood ran slower in my veins.

I'm short, five five, and a Jew, and either one of these is reason enough to get pounded. Silence fed my fear. I listened to them, and hated them right then.

The Negro's skull had been fractured, both hands had been broken, and his body was a mass of welts from chest to pelvis. The late afternoon papers reported he was in critical condition, and the entire left side of his face had been totally paralyzed.

The police had gotten a tip, however, and they tracked down two of the guys who had done the job on the kid. The boys were both taken into custody. That didn't help the Negro kid, much. He got out of the hospital in three months.

But his face, from reports, still sags a little on the left side, where it was paralyzed.

Few of the Barons were idle. Some of them had taken the tots in hand, and in vacant lots, rooftops and basements they were showing them how to fight (thus does the evil perpetuate itself). Most of them held down steady jobs; they relied on their facility as burglars and lush-muggers (bop-droppers, in the vernacular) to augment their incomes, however, for the bulk of their earnings went to the head of the family. But the *balling money* came from the sweat of their own little brows in the streets and alleys.

But during these long, electricity-filled days the Barons stayed away from school, away from their jobs, away from Ben's Candy Store—far away from any known resting place where an anxious Flyer commando group could find you. They also stayed cold away from Flyer turf, as conscientiously as the Flyers made sure not to inch over into Baron country; there was no sense pushing for unneeded trouble; there would be enough bopping shortly; and if you got caught and stomped, that was one cat less for your team when the big noise came.

And the neighborhood . . .

What of the neighborhood?

How do the older residents, the police, the storekeepers feel? Do they know what is about to happen?

The neighborhood . . .

During the days, the kids hang around the steps of the brownstones, in softly-talking groups of ten and fifteen.

95

The old women do not come out on the steps to take the sun; the lazy building-janitors stay in their cool basements, in their T-shirts, in their beard stubble, in their bottles; drugstore owners do not send out their young assistants to roll down the awnings; outdoor hot dog stands find business at a standstill; younger fathers and businessmen look tired and resigned; mothers find themselves arguing more and more with their daughters about going out; little Polish women with market bags hurry to the grocery and back, making sure they keep to well-lighted, crowded streets; people cross the avenue when a gang of kids comes around the corner.

Beer cans fall out of windows more and more frequently, and every time the clang hits the pavement, someone jumps and looks frightened.

Things tighten up; nerves fray and part.

Entering any of the neighborhoods in Flyer or Baron turf, you can feel the heat of terror, the pulse of expectancy.

Owned and protected by the gang, each member becomes part of a great illicit gestalt, and when one snaps, they all snap; when one laughs, they all laugh; when one smacks his palm with a moist fist, so do they all. It is the eggshell thinness of emotions, the throat-drying waiting.

And the police are helpless.

A Brooklyn beat cop phones in and says, "Something's wrong out here in Red Hook. I don't know what, but I think the kids are starting to shake. It might be a big rumble. Maybe we need some help out here."

So more prowl cars come in, and nothing's wrong.

Nothing at all. Not a sound, not a sight, not a drop of a pin. Nothing's wrong:

Except that the entire area is about to explode, and blood will run into the storm drains.

All that, in the rumble. The rumble, so psychologically satisfying to the immature mind of the young tough. It provides for him the adventure of an escapade that will liven up an otherwise humdrum existence. It is packed with all the drama, danger and romance the movies and TV have come to associate with war and killing. It allows him to show his stuff. It's the feudal joust, with the protection of all his buddies. No one can die ... that's the philosophy. No one can die, or really be hurt, or get stomped bad. It's the war, and right will win.

Right, in the ethic of the gang kid, is easily equatable with might. The team with the most players takes the ball game. But no one dies ...

On Sunday night, Pooch called a full meeting, and everyone showed. They had to show or be called chicken. It was the time for assigning of positions in the battle order, and every stud was afraid he would get picked for first rank, charging right into the Flyers at full strength.

I had been having strange dreams, all the week before. I'd felt something terrible would happen to me if I went on that rumble. But there wasn't much I could do about it. I had to show up ... for many reasons. Not only would I lose face with the Barons, not only would my researches come to an end, at that most crucial point when I felt I might find out my "moment of truth," a rationale for what these kids were doing to their lives, but it had grown to mean something to me personally. My strength, my own face, my status and my own personal evaluations of my courage, all of them were in my hands, to examine, to test, to finally, after all the years of wondering, know in the extreme. How would I work in the field. Would I run ... would I stand ... or would neither come to me? It was a crossroads, and I knew I had to go the route. All the way.

And there was Filene, who had come to mean quite a bit to me. We had been together almost constantly, every evening since my initiation. Kindness and even a semblance of what she thought was love had done wonders with her. She smiled frequently now, and talked, and no longer carried the halting motions and tones of a young girl afraid of the light as well as the dark. She was fast becoming a woman. I didn't want to let her down.

Candle, however, did not show. His bad standing with the club had grown so deep since our fight, that he had decided to get away from the turf and the Barons before the humiliation of official ejection could be suffered. Fat Barky, however, either through stupidity or stubbornness, was not only present, but making an ass of himself by declaring to anyone who would listen, "I'm gonna bust their asses in half!" No one doubted he could do it, they just didn't want to hear about it.

Everyone was keyed tight. There was a great deal of semi-hysterical laughter, and I could see one large group in the far corner puffing tightly, drawing down and holding, reefers and pot smoke.

Pooch was talking to Mustard and Fish, and when he saw me come in with Filene, he motioned me to join him. I told Filene to stay away from the bunch who were winging it on marijuana, and went to the Prez.

"We got trouble," he told me, as I came up to them.

I could see worry on his face, through the smoke.

"What's the matter?"

"They picked off Willyum, was goin' down to the store, some shit like that, they picked him off, don't even know where he is!" He smacked a fist into his palm.

"You wanna be War Counselor?" he finished. I stared at him, uncomprehending. *What* had happened to Willyum?

Fish turned to me; he knew me a little better than Pooch, and he clarified. "Flyers, man. They caught Willyum someway, he was goin' down to the store for his old lady and they jumped him outta'a car, he's gone, man. We don't know where."

Willyum had been one of the three head War Counselors of the Barons. He had been abducted, apparently by a Flyer trouble squad. It was a very nice trick; it had much the same effect (I'm led to understand) of killing the Chief of an attacking party of American Indians. Or something. Whatever the history of the maneuver, it had served to unnerve the Baron hierarchy, and they wanted

98

to cover before the rest of the fighting force found out. So they would slip in a new War Counselor. Me. All right, what was there to lose? All I had to do was come up with tactics, and in this social set that shouldn't be too difficult.

"Okay, I'll be a Counselor."

Pooch slugged me lightly on the arm.

Camaraderie was the order of the day.

Pooch called them to attention, finally resorting to swearing when several cliques would not cut the clamor. When they were all settled, he did his best to call the roll, and then gave them the few latest bits of information that spies and neighborhood hangers-on had been able to concoct or actually ferret out. He did not mention the missing Willyum. Then he announced me as the new War Counselor with some half-witted alibi about Willyum having to leave town with his parents. Nobody said anything, but neither did they seem to swallow the story. Willyum's parents hadn't spoken to each other in ten years; both were chasers. But I was installed as War Counselor and except for Flo, Fat Barky and several other kids whose dislike I'd engendered, it seemed to be a happy announcement.

I got some applause, and they demanded I make a speech, so I mouthed some bloody platitudes about creaming the Flyers and regaining control of bits of turf we'd lost over the years, etcetera, etcetera. It wasn't the Gettysburg Address, but it was apropos.

Pooch concluded the meeting with a stern warning to all the studs, "An' stay away from the Lucy and the shit. I don't want none of you out of action f'r t'morrow." And with that stern warning to avoid liquor and narcotics, Pooch closed the meeting.

Filene came over to me and hugged me, congratulating me on my new position in the gang, and we made to leave. Mustard grabbed my arm as I went past, and leaned over to whisper in my ear.

"We're havin' a blast over t' Flo's pad, her folks is outta town'r somethin'. Wanna make it?"

I hadn't been at a full-fledged gang brawl yet, and the

idea appealed to me. I said fine, we'd show, and Filene followed me out of the basement, and then to the street. I asked her if she wanted to go to the party and she said anywhere I went, she'd go. Since we couldn't wander the streets in that atmosphere, we sat around on the upper landing of a tenement for a half hour, not wanting to be the first ones there, and then made it up to Flo's parents' apartment, in one of the old brownstones on the Avenue. It was on the fourth floor, and from the second floor up we could hear the noise. When we knocked, the door swung inward without being opened. The smoke was so dense I could only make out forms, not faces. The sweet, sticky smell of pungent pot being smoked was high in the room. I could hear glasses clinking, and shrill screams of happy, hysterical chicks. The joint was truly swinging. Over in the corners—as my eyes grew accustomed to the smog— studs were exploring the anatomies of their Debs, and there wasn't a bare area of the room in which a person could light. Filene and I stepped over a pair of lovers necking on the floor, and around two toughs who were Indian-wrestling North Woods style. We got into the room, and Mustard came out of the kitchen with Flo on his arm. Her blouse was open to the waist.

"Hey, man!" he greeted me. I grinned back. The smell of pot was making me sick. I wanted to leave.

Filene pulled my head down and she whispered in my ear, "If Poochie finds out about this, he'll be really sore." I nodded and gave her a kiss on the cheek, trying to reassure her.

To be sure, Pooch would split a gut. He'd told them to keep away from junk and juice, and here they were getting themselves put out of commission even before the fight had started. I felt uneasy about being there, but with half the Barons in the room, it didn't figure that I'd be singled out for retribution, should Pooch make the scene. And I had a hunch Mustard and Flo and the rest had taken great care to keep Pooch in the dark.

"Where's the beer?" I asked a boy named Kurt, who

was putting a stack of 45's on the record player. He jerked a thumb toward the bathroom, and I left Filene to get us each a brew.

They had the tub filled with ice cubes, and perhaps three cases of Rheingold chilling. I took out a couple of cans and used the opener on the sink-edge, noting that the boys had started drinking early, before the beer was cold, for spray marks of warm brew were all over the wall.

I threaded my way back through the revelers (overhearing much bravado in the conversations), and handed Filene her beer.

Someone shouted happily (if a bit drunkenly) from the kitchen, and I edged to see what was happening. They were whomping up a batch of home-brewed hootch, Sneaky Pete, in there, and the pot had boiled over, further decorating the walls with slimy, off-green liquid. Pete (often strained through a loaf of rye bread to distill it), is guaranteed to put hair on a woman's chest, cause a horse to get the blind staggers and start walking backward, make a man go insane or a fruitcake stable. I've heard of Sneaky Pete turning a cat blind, and of starting another's guts to running counter-clockwise, they dug it so much.

Pooch had been wise in advising them all to stay away from artificial stimulants. He didn't want any of his good men juiced up in some alley or doorway. I took my beer, pulled Filene after me, and hunkered down just behind the door to the apartment.

About one o'clock, after we'd had two phone calls from the neighbors threatening to call the fuzz (which they would never do—they knew better), I was half-bored and half-asleep, about ready to cut out, when the door banged open by my head and the Executive Council came storming in.

Pooch came on like he was wearing seven-league boots, and had smashed half a dozen glasses of juice out of guys' hands, before they even knew he was in the room. I sat very quietly, pulling my legs into the little area behind the door, and hugging Filene close to me, trying to be as inconspicuous as possible.

Pooch caught sight of Mustard, half decked-out with a reefer in his jaw, and snapped his fingers for Fish and one of the other boys to grab him. They caught Mustard by the biceps and dragged him to his feet, dumping Flo to the floor. She just lay there. I don't know what she had been popping, but it had turned her off completely.

Fish and the other stud held Mustard up between them, and Pooch came over, grabbing a fistful of the boy's blonde hair. He dragged his head up and swept the reefer from Mustard's mouth with a backhand slap. It jarred Mustard's head and his eyes started to focus. He tried to pull loose, and the two side-boys gripped him all the tighter.

"Man, I *told* you . . ." Pooch explained.

Then he drew back his fist and drove it into Mustard's gut. He did it again. Then he did it again. He began to systematically, scientifically, beat the living crap out of one of his own War Counselors.

Everyone's attention was riveted to the scene of brutality in the far corner of the room, and I took that moment to haul Filene to her feet, and slip around the open door, out into the hall, and down the stairs.

The last thing I saw was Mustard blacking out, slipping loose between the two guards and being allowed to fall in a nasty heap. As we sneaked down the stairs, I heard Pooch's voice, vicious and compelling, advising them to, "Hit for home before the rest of you bastards get it!" We were in a doorway next to Flo's building as the rest of the party broke down the stairs and scattered in all directions.

Thus was justice meted out in the world of the kids.

I couldn't agree with the manner in which it had been dealt, but there was no denying it was the most effective way of making an example of Mustard. They would all be straight the next day.

Monday was murder. It was difficult to speak, and even more difficult to stand up. My knees had a tendency to shake, and nothing I thought or said seemed to have much validity. I'd been having the dreams again; wet, red dreams, and I was the central figure. I called my agent and spoke to him for a few minutes, telling him what was happening and how I was getting along; he sounded worried.

But not half as worried as *I* sounded.

At nine o'clock, almost as though a soundless chime had been struck in everyone's head, the full membership, including Squirt groups, Debs and allies, met in the club rooms. Pooch made a few remarks about Puertos and what we would do to them. They sounded hollow and phony. Everyone was scared witless, no matter what outer facade was worn.

Then the weapons were passed out.

Mustard, who had been in the first rank, was not on the scene. I wondered what had happened to him. I hadn't thought Pooch had mussed him up that much, but apparently his loyalty had gone South. I was ordered into the front rank of attackers. Filene's mouth went slack and her eyes became moist as she heard Pooch tell me. I didn't say anything. I was beyond complaining.

They handed out the weapons, then.

Fish gave me a .30-.30 but I handed it back. "I can do better with these," I said, pulling out a vicious pair of knucks constructed from little steel cubes mounted on an iron bar, and wound with friction tape. "And this," I showed him the bayonet.

The knife was a formidable thing, originally used by the Rangers in World War II, so constructed that it could be used to slide in between an opponent's ribs or crush his skull with the massive handle.

I had seen the knucks used by another boy. Wielded properly, they could open a jaw in five places. They were effective and impressive tools. I didn't want a gun. I didn't want to *have* to kill someone.

Fish shrugged, took the rifle, and gave it to someone else.

Mothers who are vaguely aware that their sons will some day have to go into the Army should have been there. They would have gone pale and sweaty at sight of the hungry eyes and ready hands groping toward those guns. The killer was at the surface now. No one spoke—they snarled. There is a feeling to the wood and metal of a weapon that is unlike any other. It can transform a man. And it can make boys into men in a second. The picturesque language of the gutter-kid was gone, only the obscenities were left.

... and I had the least dangerous weapons in that room.

The social workers and gang supervisors had by this time gotten word of the rumble, of course. No one, not even a blind deaf-mute, could have missed the signs. The neighborhoods were alive with tension ... no one was on the streets but strangers and fools ... cars had somehow found ways of detouring around these sections. But no one could stop it. The police knew a war was about to break, but they didn't know where, and the social workers were up against a brick wall. The squealers and adult informers had been warned about talking. This was one rumble the gangs wanted to come full force. It was the settling of many scores.

As we armed, I thought about it, briefly.

It's better, I told myself. *Don't try to break it up, don't try to stop it. A lot of cops and social workers will get hurt if you do.* Let them throw themselves at one another, these urchins with death ready. Let them smash each other, and rip and blast, let them. Let them go at it till the blood mounts up in the gutters. *They're like army ants ... no one can come before them and hope to stop them.*

The fight was inevitable: *all* their fights are inevitable, and if they aren't handled under terms of war, where many will survive, they'll do it with knives in the back and with homemade bombs in the schoolrooms, and many more will die. *So let them alone. Let them kill each other.*

Maybe the sight of all that blood will one day stop them. Maybe, some day. But not today. Today was lost.

It suddenly caught at me. I was one of them. The blood that ran might be mine. My philosophy went right out the window. *Stop them*, I thought! Stop them cold, before it's too late. I couldn't be bothered worrying about anyone else, then. I'd painted myself into a corner, and there was no way out.

And right then, I didn't have to play-act any more. I *knew* how the kids felt, with no way out of the mess.

That close to a rumble, all of us, and only an act of God could prevent the thing from happening.

And God didn't seem to be interested in any of us poor slobs.

CHAPTER NINE

Prospect Park at ten minutes to eleven was pitch-black. They had broken most of the street lights. It was really dark. And the Park was teeming with gang kids. I had laid out my particular section of the battle plans, using a simple expedient of skirmishers right and left, with an advance force holding back center, just slightly, to allow the men on either side to encircle the Flyers coming at us. Fence had his flare gun and he was in the first rank with me. I had a feeling that weapon would be highly useful in lighting up the fighting area, once we'd engaged the enemy.

We had come into the Park on foot, by a devious path, and I hadn't been settled in the bushes for more than two or three minutes before a church bell began chiming the hour. The longest, slowest, fastest eleven strokes of a chime I'd ever heard.

I can't quite think of any other way to say it, except to reiterate that I was really scared. I'd come out here to write about this thing . . . not get killed in the middle of it.

Fence was right beside me, belly-down in the dirt under that bush, the Very pistol held out stiffly before him, his hand steadying it, and its large round canister muzzle black against the darkness. Most of the others were together, save the skirmishers I'd sent out on either side. It was good gang psychology; not only did it keep the weaker wills from sprinting, but it buoyed up morale. Might is right, superiority in numbers. And yet, we had no idea how many the Flyers had been able to recruit.

There were very nearly a hundred Barons spread out through that end of the Park, all hunkered down, waiting, waiting for something to happen. I scuttled around to look behind me, out across the Avenue, and saw the main part of the fighting force coming from behind a line of parked cars. This was how the War Counselors had set it up: plant the first wave in the Park ahead of time, and let the Flyers think the main batch was all we had.

The chime struck for the last time, and the huge gang of Barons broke across the street.

The Puerto Rican Flyers were ready for them.

I had heard nothing till that moment, but now, even as the slap-slap of sneakers sounded on the street, the first shots exploded off to my right and I heard a high, adolescent voice scream in pain. Someone was a damned good sharpshooter. It had started.

The pitch-black of the park was suddenly firefly alive with gunbursts and sparklers of flame. Most of the shots were going wild, but occasionally I could hear a thrashing and a coughing in the trees. Blood seemed to be drenching me, not sweat.

Apartment windows had flown up at the first shots and cries, screams, bellows of rage floated through the bushes. The main force had taken to the underbrush. Someone in the buildings was shouting for the fuzz.

Someone else was lying under a tree, clutching his chest and "Hail Mary's" with bloody fingers and a swollen tongue.

Beside me, Fence rasped, "Now? Now I do it? Huh, now?"

I laid a hand down on his back to shut him up.

Not yet.

Let's live a little longer. Don't attract attention to us, for Christ's sake. My eyes were filled with pinpoints of light. Shots, from everywhere. The night was alive with sound. Everywhere.

I was consumed with a wave of panic. I was sorry I'd ever wanted to write about how street gangs operated. I was going to find out, in the field, but I might never live to write about it. It was no holds barred, and they liked that, as long as it was someone else who caught the slug in his throat.

Fence leaped up and started running. I tried to stop him, but he was gone, into the dark, between the trees. And my legs were under me, too, and I was running, without mind, without thoughts, just running, with that bayonet hard between my fingers and my left hand covered by the steel knucks. But I hung back, and heard movement all around me as the main force went streaming and screaming past, right into the face of horror.

First boy through the trees was caught in the eye by a long pole with a piece of glass taped to the end. His screams brought the rest running. A Deb dropped beside him and got a good look; it was her stud; she started screaming, trying to cram her fist into her mouth. I felt the adrenalin go squirting through me. I wanted to run with the pack!

I wanted to kill, too!

Like sharks smelling blood.

Go!

The zips came into play. Their sound was not as sharp and slight and clean as the rifles or hand guns. They had no accuracy, thank God, but even so, the danger was there. And I didn't know what I was doing there, just running among them, swinging that bayonet and connecting with air, just air, but wanting flesh, wanting to carve someone up, seeing myself as a dark knight in the battle, doing the most basic thing a man can do . . . fighting. It took no brains to fight, and less to die, but I had no brains . . . I was a dark knight!

A black shape heaved up out of a bush as I passed and murmured *miera,* come here, as I felt a blast of pain that

108

numbed my right arm completely. I don't know how I held onto the bayonet. I suspect I *had* to, that was why! I pulled up and swung, smashing my steel knuckle fist into the face of the guy with the heavy club. I felt his head snap around the blow, and he crumpled past my legs.

I must have kicked him a dozen times.

I grabbed the club with my left hand, awkwardly, for the knucks were still wrapped around my fist. I pulled them off and shoved them in my side pocket, hefting the club. It was a sawed-off chair leg of ironwood with a hunk of lead in the business end. It was heavier than a couple of bricks, and deadlier. It gave me range as well as effectiveness.

One of the Debs was squawking in a broken wail, and I saw two Flyer bitches working her over. One of them had a long Italian stiletto, and she was slicing up the girl with all the cool aplomb of a butcher.

I jumped them, not thinking, really, smashing at the hand that held the knife with my billy club. The girl bellowed and screamed something in Spanish. I hit the other one in the stomach, a long flat-out swing in the breasts, and then half the Flyer club was down my shirt.

Those chicks got their kicks. On me.

I went straight down and they did a rain dance on my head. I didn't wake up for quite a while.

When I did, the first thing that shot through my head was *Why am I still alive?*

I was a ball of pain, lying under a bush where someone had kicked me and not taken the time to finish me off. There must have been too many things shaking to worry about one downed Baron. I lay there, with the howling and swearing and screeching floating over my head, and the blood running down the side of my face, and my right arm useless. But I was still alive.

I was crying from the pain; but I could see. There was blood running into my eyes, and the sockets seemed to be burning, but I watched the rumble from the safety

109

of that bush. Gone to ground, all the fight out of me, so call me chicken if you will, but I wouldn't, couldn't move.

They were like wild animals. All over the place. They had been turned loose, with no one to check them, and it was Jeezus, *slaughter!*

I tried to get to my knees. I don't know why, I suppose I wanted to run away. I managed to hunker up onto one knee, and then POW! the Very pistol went off almost in front of me. The Barons were coming back the other way. They'd been routed, or were mopping up, or the damned fight was just getting sloppy, I don't know.

But that red glow lived in the sky for a minute and I saw terrified faces turned toward it. It died after a time and the trampling went on unabated. It seemed as though this thing had been going on for hours, but I knew it couldn't be. The police would have been there before that much time had elapsed. My thoughts were crazy, devoid of rationality. That socking-around I'd gotten had jazzed my brains completely.

All I could do was stare, like a nut, as they fought back and forth around me. I saw a bunch of girls, tight jeans somehow concealing vicious knives and straight-edge razors, fighting like wildcats. One girl smashed another in the breasts with a lead pipe, and kept beating her with it even after the other had fallen moaning among the leaves.

No one abroad in the Park that night would have been safe.

A body tumbled through the bushes and went sprawling, its arms and legs at funny angles, and tried to get up. It was a Flyer. He couldn't make it. He just lay there, down.

Fence was shouting something to Samson, yelling, "Hey, Sams', hey, man, hey Sams'n, help willya!"

I couldn't see them, but then the flare gun went off again, except this time it didn't explode into the sky. I saw a pulsing crimson light in among the bushes and a second later a boy came shrieking through the brush, his arms going in all directions, and his shirt-front blazing. Fence had shot him squarely in the chest with the thermite flare.

110

Oh, God, it was unbelievable. The kid went crashing past me, still burning, and out onto the Avenue, and out of sight behind the cars ... except for the glow, which kept illuminating his passage.

He disappeared down the street and in between two buildings, an erratic journey that may never have ended, or ended only when the flesh was burned away.

I felt myself clogging in the throat, and a moment later I upchucked what little I had in me. I sat there in it, and everything went grey and swam and boiled and dipped around me. It was like nothing else in this life ... totally without reason or pattern.

Then I heard the siren wail of a police growler. It was coming up the Avenue ... no, it was over there on the other side of the Park ... no, it was ... they were coming from all sides. It had taken them long enough!

I heard screams, "Leech out! The fuzz! Cut! The nabs are here!" The shouts rose up over the wails of filth and agony of the combatants. Joined in a common bond—hatred of authority, fear of apprehension and the terror of jail—they broke and ran, scattering back the way they had come, leaving their friends and brothers lying on the dew-fresh ground.

I saw Pooch, a rifle slung across his back, hanging low and scuttling through the bushes toward the Avenue.

Suddenly I was brought back to a terrifying sense of reality: I remembered my own position. I was as liable to arrest as anyone else lying there. I had to get away myself.

I dragged myself erect, clinging to the bushes, and took a step. I went right down again, flat on my face. But this time I couldn't allow myself the luxury of unconsciousness. I struggled to my feet again, and without even feeling my feet moving, ordered them to carry me away. Reflex took over. I limped through the trees, stumbling over rocks and brush and other things, keeping to the edge of the Park till I was a block down. Then I scanned the Avenue, saw nothing dangerous, and sprinted across, falling only once, scraping my hands badly on the asphalt. I gained the safety of a building's side and looked back. Patrol cars had drawn up to the curb in threes and fours. like great land-creatures, and their headlights as well as spots were flooding the darkness of the Park.

I could see the cops running into the Park and hear them dragging kids out. As I watched a cop broke out of the trees with a body over his shoulders in a fireman's carry, and another kid wrapped in his hand. by the collar. He tossed them both unceremoniously into the back seat of the growler. and shouted something to another vehicle down the line.

I heard an ambulance coming from down the Avenue.

It was going to be bad.

I slithered along the face of the building, away from the action, my arm hanging limp. burning terribly, my head filling fast with grey clouds of pain and confusion.

I ducked into the first alley I came to. between two modern apartment buildings. and followed it to its end, then over a fence and down another alley onto another street.

I don't know how long I wandered. but eventually I got back to my fleatrap room, and took a look at myself in the mirror. I had never been beautiful. but I was less so now. Half my face looked like putty, and the other half was devoid of emotion or expression.

I changed clothes after showering. and rolled up the apparel that had belonged to Cheech Beldone. As far as I was concerned. he had been killed back there in Prospect Park. I cleaned out every little thing in the room that might lead anyone back to me. I packed it all in a paper bag and left the room and the neighborhood. I caught the subway uptown, and changed at Times Square.

Eventually. years later. ages later, a whole lifetime later, I got off the subway at 116th Street across from Columbia University, and dragged myself to 611 West 114th. I got upstairs and unlocked my room, and threw the paper bag under the bed.

Then I fell down on the bed and slept.

When I woke, after hours of terrible dreams and restless tossing, I was not purged, but Cheech Beldone was gone. I was Harlan Ellison again, and I was out of Brooklyn, and off the streets. I did not know what had happened to Pooch, or Filene, or Fish or Fence or any of them. All I knew was that I was safe, and hadn't been hurt, and would never, never go back.

TRANSITION

That was the end of my first journey through hell. I was unable to write about it coherently for several months thereafter. And when I did, it was to find that I had been too completely involved for rationality. I used many of the incidents from my time with the Barons in stories, and once even attempted a complete telling of the ten weeks. It came out very badly.

Finally, I wrote a novel about it. My first novel. I called it WEB OF THE CITY and eventually it came out, under the title RUMBLE. But it wasn't a very solid book, though the reviewers were kind to it, and in its own way I suppose it said what I wanted to say, *had* to say, at that time. But there was still a feeling that I had somehow gone wrong with the concept; it hadn't been a true re-creation of the kids. Filene was not Filene, Pooch was not Pooch, and Candle came off as some sort of mongoloid, which he had never been.

Prosaically enough, time passed and things happened. I had brought away from the Barons some implements used by the kids—the set of knucks I'd used in the rumble, the billy club, a .22 revolver, the bayonet, the Italian stiletto without a switch I had used in the stand with Candle—and these were to become visual aids in lectures and panels on juvenile delinquency for PTA groups, YMCA gatherings, high school classes, youth organizations.

In 1956 I was married and in 1957 was drafted. While serving two years with the Army at Fort Knox, Kentucky, I continued to write, and lecture on juvenile delinquency, using the weapons from Brooklyn. During this latter period I lived in Kentucky and continued writing. It was during this time that RUMBLE was published, and shortly thereafter another book, a collection of short stories about delinquents I had written for various magazines. It was called THE DEADLY STREETS. On April 1st, 1959, I was released from the service and went to Chicago to edit a magazine. I was divorced in 1960, and in the late summer of that year left Chicago, returning to New York. Wandering, really. Trying to find some way to talk about the things I felt, the things I'd seen, and being still unable to set it down properly. I had sold many more stories—some of them about the kids—and several books, but nothing seemed to come out properly about how they were doomed, so helpless there in the streets. And all the while I was getting older, *they* were growing older, and their kid sisters and brothers taking over the places of the ones I had known.

What had happened to Filene, whom I had known for so short a time, yet who seemed to be a person truly loved, I had no idea. Or Pooch, who had had a strength, despite his inability to communicate; who was undeniably a man in a world that had made him too old before he was ready. Or Candle, or Fish, or Mustard, or Flo ... what had happened to them? I found my thoughts returning to them constantly, trying to imprint new images of them, older faces, new bodies, over my original pictures. I could not do it. I continued seeing them as children, looking at me, asking me to tell it already, to stop cheating them ... now that I had duped them and used them, why was I denying them their voices? Why was I hiding what I'd seen, writing it as fiction and thus negating its truth? I had no answers.

116

I kept looking in the papers, to see if I recognized any names, but for the single exception of a *Daily News* squib about a boy named Arthur "Fish" Kohler who had stolen nine cars in two days and been apprehended on his tenth, there was nothing. It might have been the Fish I'd known; I had no way of finding out.

And I was afraid, too. If they had known who I was, and I had come back on the scene after having disappeared so effectively, it might have meant serious trouble for me. Uptown, hair cut normally, suited, carrying an attaché case, I was definitely not Cheech Beldone. I was someone else entirely, and it was better that way.

And it had been seven years. A long time.

In seven years I had lectured many times on the subject; had even gone on television and radio with my experiences. I had said, "You can't stop a rumble or a kid gang once it gets rolling. There isn't much you *can* do when slums take the place of football fields, or when alleys are more convenient for loving-up a date than taking her to a canteen for dancing and clean entertainment.

"But as long as there is a solid family unit that will recognize the kid as an integral part, that will respect his intelligence, his honesty, his status, a family he can run to when the city closes down on him and the world snaps and snarls, as long as the parents and the school and the church and the local government stop looking at delinquency as a recent cultural leprosy, get off their behinds, and try to *understand* the kid, try to aid him in helping himself grow up, not shove him the way they *think* or *half-think* he should go, there's a chance.

"When everybody stops passing the buck and blaming it on girlie magazines or television or the H-bomb, then a start will be made toward solving the problem."

That's what I'd said, and showed the knives that had ripped, and the knucks that had smashed. That was what I'd said, though I'd known that wasn't the whole answer, perhaps not even the right answer.

117

But I'd known it was a start, and they had to start *somewhere*.

Sometimes it came down to insulting the parents . . .

I told them they needed to be educated, like their kids. "Honor thy father and mother" was a sweet sentiment once, but what if the father is a lush and the mother is too lazy to notice whether the stains on her son's shirt are lipstick or blood? I said, "Get the adults trained! Rid them of the idea that just because they gave birth to something they are competent to bring it up. Most parents are so incompetent they wouldn't know their kid was Public Enemy Number One unless they saw his picture in the post office."

Sometimes it came down to insulting the police . . .

"We need more beat cops. Get them out of the prowl cars. There isn't a thing they can do rolling along like conquering heroes, advertising their presence, blocks from trouble when it breaks. Let the paid servants of the people earn their pay instead of grousing about how many callouses they have on their backsides for the pittance they're paid. Pay them more. Then let the cops walk around. Then give him more cops to walk over the ground he's just covered. Blanket the rough sections. Stamp out the street mugger and the rapist and the lice that push junk to the kids. Stop the rumble by forming more youth groups, that want to let the kids help and grow, not keep them out of the way. Show them they're needed, not in the way."

Sometimes it came down to insulting the educators . . .

"You don't call what you're shoveling at kids these days education, do you? They go in stupid, and they come out stupid, if they bother going in at all. Most of them are fucking illiterate! They can't read or write or enjoy even a simple pleasure like thinking a new thought. Read a book? Like hell! Think straight enough to see through all the jingo-spouting phonies running for office or trying to sell them ass-wipe on television? Fat chance! Develop their cleverness enough to get a job that's better than sitting for

118

eight hours a day in a windowless box making money for someone else? Don't make me laugh! You program them to be no-necks; to be nerds; to take what's fed them and make no noise. Behavior mod them, brainwash teach them, scare the authority into them. You get put in a classroom with a bunch of wild animals and all you can think about is keeping them from eating your heart and eyes out. That's teaching; sure it is. You people'd be better off serving the commonweal as bricklayers."

I tried to get across the idea of action on the part of parents too busy with churchkey and time-card, action on the part of school boards too hypocritical and stingy to persuade good teachers to stay in education, action on the part of clergy and government too busy dredging up the proper indignant expressions and the proper flowery phrases for "the present outrageous situation" to get out in the streets where the kids play stickball.

I wanted them to *talk* to their kids, and to *listen*.

Many lectures, many showings of the weapons the kids used, and in seven years—nothing. The same. No change, unless it was to get worse.

So my interest turned in futility to other things. I wrote about other things, saw different scenes, and the ten weeks in 1954 began to fade.

It was all to come back to me, much more forcibly, later that month . . . September, 1960.

I had gone to a party in the Bronx, and there met a fellow named Ken Bales, someone I'd known in 1955, a fellow I'd loaned a typewriter to. He had pawned it; he had been a deadbeat then, and in 1960 he was no better. I advised him if he didn't pony up the cost of a new typer, or get me that one back, I would lean on him. That happened early in September. It was to result in an experience I never want to relive, an experience that brought back my memories of the Barons so sharply I felt I had never left Brooklyn. It happened like this . . .

119

Bales, frightened by my determination to make him pay up, and aware of the weapons I had in my apartment (locked in a filing cabinet), which had never been a secret, as I had displayed them on television, anonymously phoned the police.

He told them I had an arsenal in my Greenwich Village apartment.

On Sunday, September 11th, a hot summer day, I was doing nothing in particular, loafing around the apartment, when the bell rang. I answered it, and was confronted by two plainclothesmen of the New York Police Department. They asked if they might come in. I thought it was a gag and asked to see their tin. They showed me their credentials and I admitted them.

They were pleasant enough, sat down, and asked me if I had any enemies. I answered with a grin, and said, "I lead a normal life; I suppose I've got as many as the next guy." They didn't smile back. They asked me how long I had been living at 95 Christopher Street and if I knew of anyone in particular who would like to do me harm. I told them how long I'd been in the apartment, since I'd come in from Chicago, and the only person I could think of at the moment who disliked me enough to fink on me was Ken Bales.

Then they asked if I'd ever used narcotics.

I didn't quite know what to answer them.

Friends who knew me often thought I was a fanatic, so opposed to junk was I. A young friend of mine, in fact, had been experimenting, and a jazz critic named Ted White and I had threatened to knock his teeth in if he ever went near it again. Narcotics? Hell, no . . . I didn't even use NoDoz.

I told them I had never had anything to do with narcotics and felt this thing was going a bit too fast for me. I asked them what this was all about, and was I being charged with something. I noticed they were looking at me carefully, at my arms and my legs. I had been washing the bathroom sink at the time they had arrived and was wearing nothing but beach-boy slacks, rolled to the knees, with no shirt. They could see I had no needle marks on my body.

Then they informed me that an anonymous tip had come in to the Charles Street police station that a writer named Ellison at 95 Christopher Street was having wild narcotics parties, had a storehouse of heroin secreted in the apartment, and also had an arsenal of lethal weapons.

I knew it had been Bales, but I couldn't prove it.

At that point I asked them please to search the place. They said they had intended to do it in any case, but they were glad I'd offered so they wouldn't have to go and get a search warrant.

They spent the better part of an hour searching my one-and-a-half-room apartment, and naturally found nothing. Then they came back into the living room and sat down.

The senior officer asked me if I had a gun in the place. I had to think a moment. It did not dawn on me to equate the empty .22 short revolver I had used for seven years as a prop, with a lethal weapon that should have been registered in the State of New York. After a moment I said, "Well, I have some weapons that I've used on lecture tours, in connection with talks about juvenile delinquency." I showed them my books.

They asked if they might see the weapons.

I went to the closet, found my keys in a pair of pants, and unlocked the bottom drawer of my filing cabinet. Far in the back, under a stack of papers (for I had not been lecturing for six or eight months), I found the gun, the knife, the bayonet, and two sets of knucks. (The second set had been given to me by a student at a high school in Elizabethtown, Kentucky, after a talk I had given there, thus proving to me that j.d. was not a big city disease, solely.)

121

I handed these items over, though the bayonet and the knife (without a switch) were both legal in New York City.

They took these and I added, "I have bullets for the gun, too, if you want them." They indicated they did, so I located the box of .22 rounds and gave them to the officers, also. They smelled the gun. "When was the last time this was fired?" they asked.

"It's never been fired while I've had it," I said. "And that's seven years. Before that, I don't know." The officer with the gun nodded to the other and said it smelled clean.

We talked for another half hour, and still the seriousness of what was happening did not reach me. I was a legitimate writer with a legal use for these tools, and the whole anonymous call was a hoax, used by a kook to get me in trouble. They agreed that such might be the case, and while they were satisfied that the narcotics charge was absolutely unfounded, they would have to arrest me on the Sullivan Act for illegal possession of a gun. I thought I'd fall over, it was so weird. I'd done nothing, as far as I was concerned, and yet I was to be arrested.

They apologized, said they had no doubt I was innocent, but a complaint had been lodged, and they were compelled to follow it up. I tried to reason with them, but they were adamant in the pursuit of their duties.

I could not argue with them.

Today, I still feel I was treated fairly and honestly by those two police officers, whose names I cannot and would not reveal, for they helped me as much as they were able, later.

They advised me to get dressed, for they would have to take me in. I got panicky. My mother, whom I had not seen in over three years, had come into town from the Midwest, and had gone out for the afternoon. She would be back to make dinner in a short time. The thought of her coming in, finding me gone and not knowing where I'd disappeared—who knew how long I'd be kept in detention?—all this whirled through my mind. I asked them

122

if I might tell a friend where I'd gone. They said it was all right to do so.

I went downstairs in the building with one of the officers and told an acquaintance, Linda Solomon, what had happened to me. She thought it was a gag. "You're putting me on," she said, laughing. Then she opened the door a bit wider, saw the officer, and the smile vanished.

We made arrangements for her to tell my mother what had happened, and I went back upstairs, dressed, and left with the officers.

It was the beginning of twenty-four hours caught in the relentless mechanism of the N.Y.C. judicial system. A 24-hour period that so filled me with hopeless desperation that at times I thought I would crack.

But it was a fitting ending to my researches about the gang. For in the Tombs—New York's affectionate name for its jail—I was to encounter one of the Barons, seven years later, when I was someone else, and he was someone else, and it all tied together too terribly, too neatly, to even let me slip into the forgetfulness I'd known.

How ironic ... that a guy who had wanted to tell the truth about the kids, should be arrested seven years later as a result of having run with them. It was like the second half of a book, tied inextricably to the first by sadness and desperation and the evil that seems never to leave someone who has experienced the filth and horror of the streets.

I was going back for another visit in hell.

BOOK TWO: THE TOMBS

CHAPTER TEN

The bullpen around me was clean and bare, and filled with the naked faces of men who were guilty, except for the innocence in their hands. *See*, their hands said, as they scratched at stubbled jaws, or lay soddenly in laps, or hung outside the bars (why outside the bars?), *see, this body I'm attached to may have done evil, but I'm innocent*. The lily-white hands, so pure and free of guilt. I sat among them and wondered what I had done to get involved in this treadmill horror underneath the city of New York. I honestly thought I might go out of my mind at any moment.

From the larger marshalling room, outside the bullpen, sounds of typewriters and filing cabinets belied the fact that we were imprisoned. It sounded like an office, with busy little secretaries filing inconsequential reports. But it wasn't an office, it was the records-preparation area of the Tombs, and they were cataloguing human beings. Punch-carding and numbering them, and with each black mark made by pencil or typewriter key, the humanity of the subject vanished a little more. Reduction to symbol and file, disappearance by folio and reference number. The cold, mechanical equations of salting a man away in a cell, and knowing which cell to go to when you want him. An iron, inflexible system, prone to error that can never be

127

traced, that keeps a man in that cell or under those tons of steel and concrete for hours longer than he should be kept. The regimentation of callousness.

I could feel the entire weight of the city on me. I had been in custody for twelve hours now, and it was one automated step after another, with no opportunity to get humanity back into my actions. I was a cipher, one of a great string of bodies run through a computing system that would break me down into component parts and file me away like a piece of fruit in the proper bin.

Sitting in the bullpen, looking around me, trying to comprehend all the facets of what had befallen me, and at the same time trying to understand these others whose hands said they, too, were innocent, I was not so much a participant as a victim.

It had all happened so quickly, the arrest, the accusations, the dawning realization that this was not, indeed it was not, a hoax. All idea that this was an elaborate gag, rigged by my bohemian friends in the Village, had vanished like morning mist as the two police officers had hustled me into the unmarked squad car, and transported me to the Charles Street police station.

Now as I sat in the bullpen, grey and cold and filled with men who might have been the best or the worst of any culture— Who could tell, when the mechanical thumb of the System had pressed down on each, making each the same, all equal, all guilty save for the hands?—now I tried to recall every slightest memory and tactile sensation, every sight or snippet of sound, that had come to me since the officers had walked into my apartment.

We had gone down in the elevator at 95 Christopher, and the doorman, an easily-bought type named Jerry, was watching us with the beady ferret eyes of the short-line entrepreneur. "I've got some business to take care of, Jerry," I told him. "If my mother comes in, please ask her to call Miss Solomon." He nodded and smiled with that obsequious double-meaning known only to Manhattan doormen and bellboys. He knew something was up; I wasn't to learn till much later *how* much he had known, and how that could hang me up, nearly ruin my career . . .

They hustled me into an unmarked squad car, and started down Christopher Street to the Charles Street station house, just a few blocks away. "Hey, listen," I said, trying to get some hold on myself or the situation, "do you think I'll have to stay at the station very long?"

They tried to be helpful, and said something reassuring, but it didn't make me feel much better. I began to get the full idea that I just *might* have to be locked up for a few hours, and the prospect did not entice me.

"Are you going to mention this narcotics thing?" I asked. They gave each other a brief, knowledgeable look, and the officer driving said, "No, I don't see any reason why we have to mention it at all. I don't think there's any doubt that was a phony charge from the start."

I felt better when they said that, and decided being open with them had been the smartest course. So if they weren't going to mention the junk nonsense, and they were satisfied I had the weapons for a perfectly valid reason, why was I being taken in?

I asked them.

"Because a complaint has been lodged," they said, simply. "Someone has raised a beef upstairs, and it's filtered down to us. Now *we* have to act on it." It was my first really chilling encounter with the mindless, soulless, heartless machinery of the law as practiced in a great metropolitan area.

"We have to do our job, or *we'll* be in trouble," one of them added. I couldn't really blame them. They had homes and families to protect, too, and after all, what and who was I to them?

We arrived at the Charles Street precinct house, with the smell of the Hudson River and the docks flowing up the block to us. The Charles Street station, famed in song and story (and mentioned so notably in Gelber's play THE CONNECTION), is a great grey mass, completely blended into the surrounding warehouses and falling-down

129

buildings. It almost seems to hunker, as though it were trying to go unnoticed in the street foliage. I've gone back to look at it many times, but each time I come away from it, the details fade and merge in my mind's eye, and all that is left is that inhospitable, grey dawdling mass.

That was the building into which they took me, a stranger and terribly afraid.

We went up the steps and into the cool interior. It had been drizzling outside, a formless, slanting sadness that collected along the gutters and ran over my shoes. It seemed appropriate, somehow. Now, as we came inside, the rain still seemed to be falling indoors. I knew it was only an illusion, but the windows high and fat on the walls carried the rain like paintings. It was cool but sterile in the main hall of the station, with that faint odor of lye or detergent or whatever it is they use to keep the floors dirty-antiseptic. The front desk was shoulder-high on me, and the Sergeant behind that desk looked up with a bored, uncaring nod to the two plainclothesmen. They exchanged words and the Sergeant, holding a thick black marking pencil (almost like a manuscript pencil), jerked his thumb toward the stairs. "Take 'im up to the detective section," he said.

One of the two officers gently tapped me on the bicep and I moved between them, one in front, one behind, up the stairs to the squad room.

The squad room was perhaps sixty or seventy feet long by thirty feet wide, with a high ceiling, drab and colorless walls, a floor whose color was so grey, it must have been non-existent, and heavy light fixtures (the ones with the milk-glass globes, *you* know the kind) hanging down from the ceiling on thick chains.

Desks were scattered in a neat disorder, all across the room. Bulletin boards contained directives, circulars, wanted posters, departmental information and "cop cartoons" from various magazines. At the far left end of the room was a floor-to-ceiling barred enclosure, the "tank,"

130

where felons were summarily heaved until disposition could be made.

Two men were working at desks across from one another. One of the detectives was called by name, and the man looked up with the most everlastingly weary eyes I have ever seen.

"Hey," he said. It was a greeting, and a recognition, and not much else. The weary cop went back to his paperwork. A burst of static and some garbled code-numbers erupted from the squawk-box on the wall, but no one paid any attention. My two companions indicated a chair beside a desk, and I sat down. The two detectives who had been working at the desks looked up, almost at the same time, as though their heads had been worked by strings.

One of them said to my enforcers, "Listen, you want to hold down the fort till the Old Man gets in? We haven't had any dinner yet."

One of my cops nodded assent and the two detectives collated and tapped their papers into neat stacks, filed them away in drawers, and left the squad room. I lit a cigarette.

It wasn't bad, this waiting. There was almost a flavor of excitement about it. But I was beginning to suspect that it wasn't all going to be as simple as leaving my books with the officers and having them call me later when the matter came up. I had a suspicion I might have to spend the night in the can—but I put that thought out of my head at once . . . it was ridiculous. After all, I hadn't *done* anything.

The taller of my two friends, now free of his raincoat and carrying the paper bag with the weapons and my books, sat down behind the desk. I sat in a chair to the side of it. He looked at me for a moment, gave me a reassuring grin and reached into the desk for the forms. He wanted a statement.

I tried to think what day it was, and how old I was, and what I was doing here, and without any difficulty the answers came: September 11th, 1960 . . . twenty-six . . . I've been nabbed on the Sullivan Act, illegal possession of firearms in the city of New York, state of New York, borough of Manhattan. That was right; I knew it was right. I was ready to give him his statement.

He took it all down, including the name of Ken Bales, the fact that I had done lecture tours and been on TV with the weapons, and the additional information that I had let them search my apartment without hindrance. The detectives clued me that though this was a serious charge, he didn't think I was in much trouble.

We waited for the Old Man, the Captain.

The other two cops who had been in the squad room when we'd arrived did not come back. I assumed they'd gone off duty. While we waited, Linda Solomon arrived at the station house, and was sent up to the squad room. She had brought me a toothbrush, a tube of Gleem, some money, my reading glasses, a bar of soap, and three books:

NOSTROMO by Joseph Conrad
THE WIZARD OF OZ by L. Frank Baum
EICHMANN: THE MAN AND HIS CRIMES

I sometimes wonder about my friends.

I took the paper bag of goodies, noting the titles of the three paperbacks and grimacing strangely at her rather morbid sense of humor. She grinned back like the large Cheshire she resembles, and shrugged eloquently. She wanted to hang around and "soak up the atmosphere" of prison, but my temper had frayed by that time and I suggested not too politely—despite her kindness of trudging over in the rain with my belongings—that she get the hell out of there before they began examining her butt for needle marks.

She gave me a sisterly kiss on the forehead and advised me to keep a stiff upper. Or something in that category. *Jeezus, I wanted to get out of there.*

Perhaps forty-five minutes later, the Captain arrived. A tall and muscular fellow with kind features, he ushered me into his office, and proceeded to read my statement, checking points for clarification from time to time. He called in the senior of the two detectives who had arrested me, and asked him a number of questions about my personal behavior. The detective gave him a faithful, concise account of what had happened. Then he showed the Captain my books. Thus far I seemed to be doing okay.

I got the impression that the Captain would rather not have been troubled with me, as it was fairly obvious by that time that I was not an ax murderer, a narcotics pusher or an exposer of privates in playgrounds. But the complaint had been filed, and he was duty-bound to follow it up.

The report read, the Captain looked at me and asked me if I had any idea how the police had been put onto this matter. I told him about Ken Bales. He didn't say anything. It was obvious: the call had been anonymous, and there was no way of proving if it had been Bales or someone else. I had never thought of that . . . someone else.

The names raced through my mind. All the petty enemies a guy can make in a lifetime, the stupid ones, mostly, who would take such a punk, cowardly way to get even with someone. And then I considered a name I had not offered up before. My ex-wife, Charlotte, now living in New York, in the Bronx. Could it have been her? I didn't want to think about it too hard. I didn't want to think anyone I'd known so intimately could hate me so completely. I tried to think of other things.

After several hours of sitting, waiting, in the squad room (and I must offer truth where it comes; the Captain did not put me into the barred tank, where he could by all rights have stashed me); the Captain told me I'd have to be booked, printed, and put in a cell for the night. I was panic-stricken. They had taken the revolver, to check it out, to see if it matched up with any unsolved cases of shootings they had had in the recent past, but I thought, right up to that moment, that I would be allowed to go home, to be called up whenever the case came to court.

But the silent, deadly machinery of the law had begun

to grind, and caught in its yearning wheels and cogs, I was trapped till the cycle had run its course.

I had vivid images of my two years in the Army, and the almost pathological terror I had of being regimented, being ordered and confined, not allowed to act or speak or function as I wanted. But this was a thousand times worse. I was being locked up.

They printed me, then, and the black stains on the fingers were a visible pronouncement of my guilt, even before I'd been tried. There was one more indignity. They had no soap to wash off the black ink from the pad. A coarse paper towel merely smudged and deadened, ingrained the ink. I took to staring at my fingers, all through that night, and it was a feeling I cannot readily express.

A feeling of having been imprinted by my Times, by people who did not know me, who couldn't care less about me, who only knew that ten fingers deserved ten blots on them. "Can I have some soap?" I asked them, and they stared at me as though I was a trifle insane. "It'll wash off soon enough," they said, without comprehension.

I had been turned into a criminal by the simple act of blackening my fingers. I could see it beginning: the studied process that can take a teen-age gang kid with too much rebellion in him, and make him into something else ... a loser, a thief, a kid with inked fingers.

There wasn't any use trying to explain to them—they would have commiserated, but never understood. No one really *can* understand how an individual feels about something so personal. To maybe only one out of a million people would the sight of ink on the fingers be comprehensible as stigmata. But my heart sank.

It was to sink even lower during the next hours.

They took me downstairs and booked me. Complaint 1897, Police Ledger for Charles Street station. Booked on the Sullivan. I was now officially and forever listed in the records of the New York Police Department.

(I was to find out only months later that though the

complaint may be dismissed eventually, and the prints and mug shots requested from the Police Department, though they may in effect say the records have been struck from the files, they never are. Once printed, once catalogued, you are there till the day you die. You have a record. This is one of the unsung attributes of the often-over-zealous New York Police Department. Many innocent men have their faces in mug books in the five boroughs.)

Then I was taken back upstairs, and turned over to a guard for placement in a cell. They took me through the huge grey fire door, and down the row of tiny gun-metal grey cells, and stopped before one. Another guard down the line released the master control of the bank of cages, and the man beside me opened the individual cell with his key. I took a step forward, and stopped. I turned to the detective who had arrested me and I suppose the look on my face was mournful as I said, "Uh, hey, uh, how about if I don't uh have to go into here tonight, uh, maybe I could sit up in the uh the room back there, huh?" The detective tried to be gentle, but firm. He shook his head.

The guard was not quite so pleasant. "C'mon, kid, c'mon, get your ass in there, I haven't got all night!"

It *was* night by that time.

And getting darker every minute.

I stepped inside the cell. The guard said, "Gimme your belt and tie and that bag of stuff."

I asked to keep the books and my cigarettes and lighter, and he was about to refuse when the detective intervened. "Let him have them," he said. The guard gave him a piercing, altogether unfriendly look, the sort of look a lackey gives an official, and let me keep everything but my lighter. I had to light one cigarette and keep smoking all night if I wanted nicotine. Chain smoking. All night.

The guard slid the door shut and I heard the master bar slam home. The detective said something reassuring, something about coming for me early the next morning and I should try to get some sleep. I grinned mawkishly and

135

said, "Helluva hotel you've got here." He grinned back, and went away.

The guard stayed and stared at me for a few more seconds, trying to figure out what my pull was, that I had the plainclothes bulls going for me. Then he put my bag of goodies (which I now recall had some fruit and chicken in it, that my mother had sent with Linda) on the window ledge outside the cell, across the thin corridor . . . and he walked back the way he had come.

The light in the corridor stayed on, the fire door slammed with a J. Arthur Rank clang, and I was all alone in the tier.

It *was* night by that time.

And getting darker every minute.

I smoked.

CHAPTER ELEVEN

The cell overnight. A cell, whose dimensions, with handles attached, would have made a fine coffin. Gun-metal grey, faceless grey, cadaverous grey, emptily grey, without even the humanity of a chipped place on the wall. Solid, unbroken grey, with privy obscenities inscribed. (How? No pencils in perdition.) Durance vile with a lidless toilet that cannot be flushed. Coventry with a flat hardwood bedslab and a light that never goes out.

That light. All night in my eyes. Was this a modern American jail or a stopover on the Brainwash Express? I expected the Cominform representatives at any moment, with subtle thumbscrew tortures unless I revealed the plans for the Yankee spaceship. Jeezus, that goddam bulb . . . no wonder they encased it in a hard-glass shield, and a wire mesh, so no one could break it. They may have been afraid of some pistolero smashing it to obtain a sharp shard of glass to aid an escape, but in my case all I wanted to do was get some sleep, and that sonofabitch was burning out my eye-sockets.

I spent the night for the most part awake; there was no sleeping with the light in my eyes. That isn't entirely correct. A lesson well-learned in the Army was: When they yell *fall out*, shuck out of your pack, use it for a pillow and drop where you are.

I could sleep in a rock field, within a matter of seconds be completely out of it. But I couldn't sleep that night. It wasn't the bulb, entirely. It was where I was sleeping.

Part of the time I read. Enchanted as generations of tots and elders have been by Frank Baum's Dorothy and Tin Woodman and Scarecrow and Wizard, none of them could have blessed the kindly old characters as much as I did that night. They took me out of myself, and I recognized for the first time the full value of fantasy. But eventually I had to think about it. I had to put one of the smoking cigarettes on the edge of the toilet bowl in my mouth, close the book, and sit on the edge of that hardwood slab, and think about it:

Was I guilty? I didn't for a moment consider myself guilty in the accepted cultural sense of the word. I had committed no crime, and had in fact come by the weapons as a result of trying to do good, of trying to mirror a true state of our times. But in the deeper, moral sense, was I responsible for my actions, was I in prison rightfully? I had to know. I had to reason it out as a human being; I had to analyze my own ethics and morality, and decide if being behind bars was proper in this instance.

And so I considered it, silently, for a long time. I had, indeed, run with a gang, for purposes which I chose to consider altruistic and lofty. But had my own personal needs for recognition and stature dictated my course? Was I really a *dilettante*, who took his chances when he thought he could get away without being punished . . . or was I completely honest about my motives? I discounted the word "completely." No one is ever completely anything.

Finally, I decided that it was neither all black nor all white. I was partially guilty, of selling out my responsibility to the kids I had seen in the streets, by writing cheap blood-and-guts yarns about them, rather than going the longer, harder haul and doing it sociologically. But though I was guilty of moral turpitude in varying degrees, I was not guilty of selling out my society. I had prostituted my talent to make money—for many reasons; most of which

138

(wife, home, three squares a day, a few primary pleasures, a little class) would not be considered improper by the majority—but the crime was in my soul, not in my dossier.

Guilty? Yes, of selling out, of obfuscating, of cheapening my message, of dawdling and playing the *poseur*.

But guilty of owning a lethal weapon with intent to perform a crime . . . of indulging in illegal activity . . . of corruption in the greater sense . . . no, never.

I went back to the Land of Oz with a pastel heart, with an ease and peace. I hadn't turned to obsidian as yet. Soon, perhaps, here in hell, but not just at the moment. At the moment I was a flawed human being, a man with imperfections, a little guy who wanted desperately to be a big guy. But I wasn't a criminal. Not yet. Not just yet.

Still, I didn't read about Eichmann that night.

Sometime after three-thirty I fell asleep. I might have liked to report that it was a night filled with dark phantasmagoric shapes, threatening, but nonesuch was the case. The Army had taught me well. I slept like a baby. When I came back from wherever it was I had gone, the morning had come through the window across the corridor, the light had gone out, and I was stiff as a bitch. My right shoulder felt as though someone had gone at it with a piton. Several vertebrae were ratcheted sidewise, and I had that next-day feeling of mugginess, with my nose and eyes and ears filled with moist, unpleasant, viscous matter. I could not wash, not just then, and I felt like hell. Eyes grainy and chin stubbly, suit wrinkled from having used the jacket as a pillow and the pants as sheets, hair mussed and lank from the high temperature, I looked the part of a seedy street-bum, brought to bay.

I heard noises and the fire door opened down the line. The guard came in, followed by one of the detectives who had arrested me the late afternoon before. They came up to the cage and we went through the unlocking procedure.

The guard told me I'd have time to wash up later, but right now I should get my can in gear.

I followed the detective downstairs, and as we walked, he said, "Look, I'm supposed to put the cuffs on you, but I don't think they're necessary, so when we get downstairs, I'll be going in my car, following you."

"What am I going in?" I asked.

"The wagon," he said.

"Where?"

He jerked a thumb downtown. "One hundred Centre Street," he replied. I believe I must have said something, because he took me under the elbow and steered me down the stairs, saying, "Listen, take it easy. The judge'll be very easy on you. The Old Man didn't let us down, and he agreed on not mentioning this junk charge. So you won't have any real problems."

I hoped not. I had asked Linda to get in touch with my agent, Theron Raines of the Ann Elmo Literary Agency, in order to prepare bail if it was needed, though the general consensus had been that all I'd need was remanding into my own custody. The books I'd written had apparently given me some small stature as a reputable member of the community.

Charles Street station had been quiet the night before. I was the only passenger in the meat wagon. They hustled me into the back, and locked the grilled door. I sat there, finger-combing my hair and clutching my little bag of goodies to me. As the wagon started, I fished out a chicken leg and began chewing on it.

We went careening through downtown New York, with the city going away from me in a grilled panorama, the people staring in when the wagon stopped for lights, seeing what I'm sure they considered The True Face of Evil.

I tried to look young and innocent.

It was still drizzling, and the day itself was cold and handmaiden to misery. You had to walk slanting forward into the wind to make any progress. People were huddled like indeterminate clots of mucus in the doorways, and only occasionally would a hardy soul burst from under an awning to streak for other refuges. It was a nasty, unhappy day, and I was going to jail.

I hoped my agent would be in court with the bail money.

The desperation I had known at odd moments through the night, the desperation at being totally confined, had passed with my entering the wagon and its scene of freedom just beyond the grilled enclosure. But I knew that when I was hustled into 100 Centre Street it would begin again, only much worse, for then I would be in the stomach of the great inhuman processing machine of the government, not isolated (where humanity and freedom from total cynicism still existed) in one of its far-flung outposts.

We pulled up in front of 100 Centre after spiralling down through Wall Street and the heart, guts, liver & lights of the insurance, legal, bonding and stock-broking sections. I had ridden alone the whole trip, but now, as I jumped down from the truck into the waiting hands of my arresting officer, I joined a stream of sodden humanity that poured through the back-basement door into the Criminal Courts Building, the outer layer of the Tombs.

I was first remanded to the custody of a bench in a large waiting-room. There were fifteen other men, dotted back through the rows, also waiting. I tried to look at them, to study them, without seeming surreptitious. The predominance of Negroes was striking, perhaps because of the infrequency of a white face. But all of the men in the room had one thing in common: shabbiness.

These were the epidermis of society, scraped off the sidewalks and bar rails and tenement stairways and gutters of the late night and early morning. They slouched or leaned in their seats, eyes sticky with black dirt and wasted hours, merely waiting to be nudged, chivvied, harried and pushed through this seemingly too-familiar routine. I shuddered just a little to think anyone could allow himself

141

to lose all dignity in this way. And then I caught myself, chiding myself on such näive, provincial thinking. Men do what they can do, and when the culture asks them to be what they cannot be, they fall. These were the fallen ones, on whom pity would be not only wasted, but vilified.

My name was called from beyond a floor-to-ceiling grilled door, and my detective appeared in the shadows on the other side. "C'mon, Harlan," he urged, and I rose.

They opened the grilled gate for me, and I was immediately surrounded by camera equipment. Great hanging booms and pedestaled shutter-boxes, coils of boa-thick rubber cable and batteries of Kleig lights. I was about to be mugged, having already been printed. My picture was about to go on file in the endless drawers of the Law. How wonderful! I felt like doing a little native dance of pleasure that now I was in the same scrapbook with "Legs" Diamond, John Dillinger, Baby Face Nelson, Al Capone and all the other folk-heroes I had watched James Cagney and Paul Muni and George Raft impersonate on the silver screen, Saturday afternoon in Painesville, Ohio. How wonderful to come twenty-six years and have reached such a pinnacle of success. *You're just bitter*, I heard myself thinking, and replied very honestly: *What gave you your first clue, Dick Tracy?*

They sat me down on a stool. I was too low.

"Spin the seat for the dwarf," the comedian on the other side of the camera said.

Somebody else nudged me to move, so hard I almost went sprawling. "Take it easy on him," said my detective from the darkness. (Already I had identified him with Good and Daddy and Safety and Kindness.)

"Oh," the cameraman drawled the word out with meaning, "is *that* The Author?" The detective laughed lightly, and behind me, the schmuck who was spinning the black-enameled-top stool was simpering like a fag.

So that was my stir-name. The Author.

Sound of audience reaction, mildly upheaving.

"Awright," said the yo-yo behind me, "siddown."

I saddown and the man with the daguerreotypes said much too loudly, "Ah, hold your chin up there, Author, we're takin' this for the next book you write . . . ya gonna send us a copy?"

"Why the hell don't you stop making like Mickey Mouse and just take your little pictures, hero?" I said it and got a crack across the nape of my neck for my trouble. I started to spin on the stool, but my detective yelled, "Okay, just sit there, Ellison, and don't give anyone any trouble."

I saw my images of Daddy shatter. It didn't matter who was right or wrong; Negroes hang with Negroes, Jews hang with Jews, Catholics hang with Catholics, and cops hang with cops. If blood is thicker than water, how much thicker is tin than blood?

He snapped the photos (I neglected to mention they had hung a board with numbers around my neck, suspended from a chain. It wasn't heavy, but there is something so inhuman about being reduced to numbers that defies description. But I digress . . .) and my detective came over to remove the numbered slate. He needn't have bothered. I had it off a second after the last photo was snapped.

I followed him, still clutching my little bag of almost-gone goodies, and books, and we went into another room, and up a slight incline. There were twenty or twenty-five men waiting, accompanied by one or more arresting officers. They clotted in a mass near a heavy door leading to the street. The door was open, and I could see steps leading up, a black banister, the sidewalk, and a score of meat wagons. This was the transportation to the Court House building just down the street.

My officer began talking to another detective, and they discussed inconsequentialities for a time, until some invisible signal was given (I suspect it was the reaching of a group total, as other prisoners had been added to our group from the photographic section every few minutes) and we started to move out to the wagons.

It was then that my detective took out his handcuffs

143

and snapped one of the bracelets around my left wrist. He pulled over his friend's prisoner, and hooked us together. I stared down at my manacled wrist, and suddenly felt myself trapped worse than I had at any point in the events of the past day. I tried to shake loose, but both detectives shoved me forward with my arm-partner, and we joined the regimented line of men going to court.

It was still raining, and much harder now, with a sad granite look to the sky, hard and dappled grey and infinitely oppressive. The wind caught at my face and at my coat, and it was cold, terribly cold, and not all of it was from outside. My insides were cold, as well; chilled through to the marrow, as the men ahead of us clambered into the wagon, and my chain-buddy made to follow.

He jumped slightly and gained the back of the wagon, pulling me up roughly with him. The manacle bit into my wrist. "Hey, take it easy," I howled. He didn't say anything, just gave me a look of such utter contempt that I was forced into silence.

I was the last one in the truck, the door was closed, and a uniformed cop climbed onto the back step, clinging to the rails on either side. He stared in at us. Most of the men paid no attention. I looked at them, trying to decide whether they were good men gone wrong, victims of circumstance like myself, or hardened criminals.

Aside from the derelicts, with their shabby clothes and fetid breath, we all looked pretty much the same. If they had been mass murderers, I would not have been able to tell them from offenders with too many parking tickets. Abruptly, the wagon lurched forward, and we moved out of the little alley behind 100 Centre.

I could not see where we were going, for the cop on the back step blocked the view, but it didn't matter, for as we were shifting and moving on our benches, trying to get some small measure of ease for gluteus muscles doomed to hard cots and metal slabs, my cuff-buddy turned to me and asked: "What'd they get 'choo for?"

I studied his face for a moment, seeing little more than

lank hair and a wide elfish mouth, cold and empty grey eyes and ears that stood out a trifle too much from his head. I was about to answer, when I realized that his white shirt was not merely ripped and dirty, as I had at first supposed—there is a tendency not to look at your companions too closely, when in jail—but was torn down across his left arm, exposing it to the shoulder, and the dark brown stains all across the face of the shirt were most certainly blood. Great clots of blood. Hardened spittle strings of blood. Spatters and patches and gouts of blood. He was dappled in blood, from neck to waist. I swallowed heavily.

"I, uh, I had a gun," I said simply.

There was no desire in me to engage this man in conversation. I had the most terrible feeling that he was one of the true animals, not merely a *schmuck* like me, who had about as much right being in a paddy wagon as Porky Pig. I did not want to say anything to him. And that was why I heard myself asking, "Why'd they arrest *you?*"

He sneered down at me, and his nostrils flared, giving him an oddly Semitic appearance for a moment.

"I done somethin' worsen you with that gun," he said. And then he clucked like a chicken. "Heh, you betcha I did . . ." He clucked again several times, and I supposed he was laughing.

I felt a nudge in my side, and a whiskery derelict on my right leaned in to pass his foul breath over my face as he confided, "He used a hammer onna little girl; he's a mean sonofabitch, don't get too close to him, or he might go nuts again."

I turned back to my companion, staring at him like some new species of life. My curiosity got the better of me, and I asked him, "Is it true you killed a girl with a hammer?"

His head snapped around and his nostrils flared wide again. "Whadjoo say? Whadjoo say t' me?" He looked like he wanted to club me down. I asked him again, very quietly, trying to soothe him, because I was scared witless,

145

but didn't see how I could ignore his red-rimmed eyes, staring at me accusingly.

"Yeah, I used a hammer onner, yeah I did, sure! All I wanted was a little piece of trim, just a little pieceah ass, at'sall. Little bitch, fourteen anna bitch, it's her fault I'm here, an' they gonna slap *me* away, frigging buncha scuts . . ." and he lurched forward, not at me, but across the aisle at two men I had assumed were also prisoners, though they were better-dressed than the rest of us.

The two men across the way moved as one, grabbing the hammer-murderer by a shoulder with their free hands, dragging their bracelet-partners partway with them.

They shoved the maniac back in his seat, and I realized they were plainclothes detectives.

I sat there, chained to a hammer-murderer who had killed a fourteen-year-old girl because she wouldn't "give out with a little trim," and felt my composure slipping . . .

My agent *had* to be there with the bail money, he just *had* to be. The night in the cell, the black smudges on my hands, the pushing and shoving and moving like cattle in a pen, it had to end at the court, or I might not be able to write about it.

I might go as mad as the poor sonofabitch chained to me. And right then I knew what James Baldwin meant when he said we are all brothers. There was much of that killer in me, and much of my innocence in him.

We *were* brothers, chained together by more than steel links.

Suddenly, I did not want to know my fellow man any better.

CHAPTER TWELVE

From then on, reality was someone else's word. What buildings I was trundled through, what men I saw passing before me and what others with whom I was cuffed, all of them and all of it were a mottled, technicolored panorama. None of it was really happening. It had been a lark, to a great degree, this being arrested, going to court, spending the night in a clean cell in the Village.

And the half dozen cliché remarks: "Well, this'll be a good way to get experience for a book, Author." That had been part of it, too. I had had stature. But what stature is there in being chained to a mad-eyed animal who had used a hammer on a fourteen-year-old girl? What kind of importance is there in seeing another human being so gone in his own sickness and depravity that even pity is wasted on him?

I tried to consider what it might be like for a young teen-ager, perhaps one of the kids from the Barons, pinched for rumbling or breaking and entering. What would it be like for him to be chained to a man such as my murderer? Would he feel the same sophisticated revulsion or would his be merely a näive sidewise-shine at a glamorous figure, a real honest-to-God murderer? I could see the fallacy of a system where the relatively innocent and the monstrously guilty are thrown together. My concern was

147

not for myself, nor even my delicate sensibilities—more often bruised than I care to admit—but simply for the thought of all the ones gone before, and all the ones yet to come, who would ride in my seat in this paddy wagon, with the darkness closing in around them.

My thoughts ceased as we arrived at the Criminal Courts Building, borough of Manhattan. (To this day I am unsure whether we were taken to another part of the same building, or into another structure entirely. Part of the eeriness and feeling of entrapment results from the sameness of the surroundings. You begin to feel you have been "inside" this great beast for a very long while, time ceases, all walls are the same wall, all eyes dead, and all hope lost. You are in the belly of the creature, and it treats you like any other morsel of food. Hope does not run in the beast's bloodstream.)

We were chivvied out of the wagon, and my arresting officer took a position to the rear of the men herding us. They began pushing and shoving us into a doorway, using phrases like, "Awright, c'mon, heyyy-*up!* Move on there, c'mon, tchip-tchip, move, g'wan . . ." almost as though we were cattle or pigs, moving down a running-trough. I expected at any moment one of them would stop us with a simple, "Whoahh!"

Then came a series of twisting corridors, white walls, large barred rooms, through which we moved, till we came into a hallway, and I saw a freight elevator.

The operator was waiting, and the entire group of us herded together. We went upstairs smoothly, the operator talking to one of the harness bulls about some minor official and his new demands on the Force. We reached our destination. (There was no way for me to identify what floor we were on: we'd been so tightly crowded that I was facing the back of the elevator.)

I managed to elbow around, and we moved out, each of us chained together, and myself being dragged slightly by the man with the hammer.

As we passed down a very narrow neck-corridor, I saw

148

a beefy and florid, bored and disgruntled-looking guard in uniform, at the end of the passage. He stood by a lectern-like wooden desk, with a huge ledger open on its top. I had an insane vision of myself signing in as a guest, or registering to vote, or making an appearance on "What's My Line?"

Q: ARE YOU SELF-EMPLOYED?

A: Yes, I'm a gun-runner and narcotics addict.

Q: ARE YOU BIGGER THAN A BREAD-BOX?

A: Here in prison, I'm smaller than a maggot.

Q: DO YOU MAKE PEOPLE HAPPY?

A: Why should I; no one makes *me* happy!

I didn't go on with that train of thought. In that direction lies madness, I suspect. But as we came abreast of the guard, my detective took me aside, and unlocked the cuffs. He took the metal bracelets off the maniac, too, and nudged him back into the stream of prisoners passing the desk, rounding a corner, and disappearing.

"This is my Author," said the plainclothesman who had arrested me the day before. "He's a good kid, so take care of him."

"So ..." said the guard, his little brown eyes coming alive for the first time, "this is The Author I've been hearing about on the radio . . ."

For a moment it didn't sink in.

Radio? What radio? The police wave-length?

"What radio?" I asked him. My detective passed me smoothly into the guard's custody.

"Oh, there was something on the early morning news about your being picked up," my detective said. He didn't elaborate, and I moved off with the guard in something of a trance.

It was the first suspicion I'd had that my arrest was not strictly confined to the police and the few chosen friends Linda would tell. It was the first suspicion I'd had that someone had spilled the news to the papers.

I wasn't to learn till much later who it had been.

Around the corner was a cell, a minor bullpen, a waiting station for the accused before they were taken to the courtroom for arraignment. It was now eight-thirty, and as yet I'd had nothing to eat, save what I'd been able to gorge down from my bag of goodies. I had emptied the paper bag into the pockets of my trench coat, and they bulged with toothbrush, paste, and books, I still felt scuffy, and unclean, and as the turnkey opened the cell door, I asked him, "Is there any place I can wash up?" He didn't even bother to answer. His keys on their chain were massive, and in his massive hand they seemed to fit. I walked into the cell, and got the once-over from my teammates. The cell was packed, with tired men, unhappy men, spade cats and ofay, handsome men and warped-looking creatures, sick guys lying on their sides on the cement floor, and jaunty swinging hipsters with knees pulled up on the bench, chewing gum and laughing to themselves. It was an early morning roust, a gathering of all the flotsam from Manhattan's streets of the night before. This was the weekend wastebasket dumpings, the guys who had had too much to drink, and the ones who had not had enough to spend, and the ones who came up short one way or another. Like me. I walked around the big cell, stepping over some of the inmates who were catching up on their sleep, busy stacking Z's in preparation for the scenes later in the day.

It was bigger than it seemed, perhaps thirty-five feet long by ten feet wide, with a little heavy metal dividing partition at one end that screened the urinal from the sight of the others. A sink was fastened to that partition, and if you pushed the button hard enough, water came.

There were already twenty-five or thirty men in the cell, and they had taken all the space on the metal bench. So I stood. And walked. I paced, and hung my hands outside the bars (Why outside, why always outside?) and studied my fellow inmates. I saw all the faces, and I wondered

150

which were the guilty and which the *schmucks* who had stepped over the line just enough to incur some cop's wrath. They certainly seemed a rabid lot ... but then, how did I look to them?

Against one wall a tall man in an Italian silk suit leaned toward his companion, a swarthy type with too much hair, badly cut, and falling down into his face as though he had scuffled with someone and had not had time to comb it. They talked in subdued tones and though I couldn't make out what their subject was, I knew the sharp dresser was bugged at the olive-skinned one about a slip-up somewhere in the recent past. Their conversation reached such a pitch of intensity—while maintaining the same level of quiet— that the sharp dresser gave the smaller felon a slap across the forehead with his palm. I looked away and passed on to a huge, muscular Negro with a cast in his right eye, sitting at the end of the bench, his T-shirt ripped halfway across the chest, revealing heavy musculature, beaded with sweat. He caught me looking at him, and there was such a return glare of hatred, that I turned away.

Lying on the floor, tossed up on himself like a fetus, I saw a man wrapped in his overcoat, clutching his knees to his chest, and snoring fitfully. Next to him, also lying on the floor, was a young man of indeterminate age—but not much over twenty-eight—covered with blood and home-made bandages. His head was swathed in them, covering the left ear and swinging down over the left eye. His cheek had a ragged cut on it, and his hands looked as though he had tried to grab a knife away from someone. His hands were ribboned with slices, hastily-bandaged with handkerchiefs, soaked through darkly. Or perhaps some-one had been trying to get the knife from *him*.

A drunken derelict lay huddled against the bars, one arm hanging out into the corridor, vomit all around him and his fellows as far away as they could get.

A terribly thin man with no jacket, and suspenders criss-crossing over the top of his long-johns, was wrapped in on himself, sitting on the bench, other men pressed in

151

on him tightly, and he shivered. He shook like a bridge-guy wire in a heavy gale, and his eyes kept rolling up in his head, showing blue-veined eyeballs. I may have been wrong (though the bird-tracks up his bare arms told me I was right), but he looked like a junkie going into withdrawal.

There were more, but suddenly I stopped looking at all of them, and settled on just one. A boy, early twenties, with a look of defiance and contempt mixed with helplessness and utter fear. I knew I knew that boy. No, not *that* boy, but another boy, someone younger perhaps? Or, someone *like* this boy, or . . . then I recognized him. It didn't seem possible . . . and yet, how great could the odds be? It was Pooch. The Prez of the Barons, here in the Tombs with me, his Boswell. Here we were, how many years later? Seven? It seemed a lifetime. I'd had two years in the Army, the slow torture of a marriage gone bad, a year in Chicago, moral and emotional decay, a comeback and flight back to my New York, months of poverty and the inability to write, a new spate of sales, this arrest, and now, full circle. I was back with the gang. I was still a j.d. and no matter what I had considered myself, we—Pooch and me—had wound up at the same place at the same time.

What were the odds?

No more than a million to one, which is about par for Dumb Fate. There had been many kids in the gang, and the odds of one of them being arrested in the borough of Manhattan (rather than home turf, Brooklyn) the same day I had been arrested, was not that strange. I looked at him, and the years had done their work.

He was still Pooch, with the thin white face and the dark hollows in his cheeks, and the oily curly hair and the bits of anthracite for eyes. But now there were character lines around his eyes, and down his face alongside his mouth. Bitter lines that were not from laughing, and not from scowling. They were from squinting, measuring the

152

angles. His hands were blockier, and his body seemed more tensed, but he was still the same kid.

I had two cigarettes left, and asked the guy in the turtle-neck sweater next to me by the sink for a light. He gave me a match, and I lit both butts. I walked over to Pooch where he sat on the bench, lost in his own brooding, and stuck one of the cigarettes down under his nose. He looked up sharply, frantically, and for a minute there was no recognition. He stared at the cigarette as though I was trying to pick a fight.

"What's the matter, Pooch," I said, quietly, "isn't it your brand?" He stared from the cigarette to me and back again, and I could see his mind working, trying to make who I was. Where had he seen this little guy? Where? Whoever it was, he hadn't seen him dressed like this ... who?

"Remember Candle, and Fish, and Flo, and Filene, and . . ."

"Cheech!"

I grinned at him and offered the butt again. "The same." He took the cigarette slowly, and tried to get a handle on whether the last time we'd seen each other he'd been for or against me. I could see him casting back through time with difficulty. The days were too much alike, the years too conformed for much differentiation, but he knew me. He knew I'd gone away, and who I had been when I'd been in his gang.

"I'll be goddammed," he said, rising from the bench. Before he had moved three steps away, an old man had slid into Pooch's seat. I drew the boy away from the others, to the angle corner of bars and sink. We leaned toward each other and puffed on our cigarettes. We didn't say anything for a while, just gauging each other, noting the changes, seeing what was to be seen.

Finally, Pooch said, "What's shakin', man?"

I shrugged, a peculiarly bizarre gesture in my suit and trenchcoat, geared as it was to leather jacket and T-shirt circumstances. "Nothin's shakin' but the leaves on the trees," I answered. He gave me a quirk of a smile.

"Helluva place to find *you,* man." He meant it, too. "You seemed sharper than that." I shrugged again; who can explain how a guy winds up in the can?

"How long's it been?" he asked.

"It's about seven now," I ventured.

He nodded agreement, then shrugged and made a weary gesture. "The slammer, man. Wow." I nodded agreement with *his* agreement. The eloquence, the beautiful eloquence of that nod, that shrug, that weary gesture! How complete! He had told me, in one shrug and a half-formed gesture, that all the years between had been wasted years, had brought him unerringly to this end-residence, as it had been ordained.

He was truly hung-up.

I started to ask him what had happened to the kids—in particular Fish and Filene—when the beefy, bored guard came into sight around the corner.

"Awright, you crumbs, on yer feet, let's move out in snappy style here!"

He unlocked the barred entrance, and some of the more drunken inhabitants tried to elbow past him. He straight-armed them back into the bullpen, and bellowed, "Awright, you buncha shits, wait a minnit!" Then he began reading from a clipboard that had been tucked under his arm:

"Alberts, Charles; Arthur, John; Asten, Clyde; Becker, Wilhelm; Brookes, John; Brown, Tom; Brown, Virgil; Brown, Wallace; Brown, Whitney; Czelowitz, August; Dempsey—"

He went on reading the names, and my name came up, and I moved away from Pooch, murmuring, "See you later." Those whose names had been called began to file out of the cell, and made a ragged line around the corner toward the elevator. I didn't see my plainclothesman, but I knew he'd be along any time now. I was both relieved and flattered when he came out of a side door in the narrow corridor; he had obviously taken a liking to me, and wasn't ready to let me sink into the System completely. Either that, or they thought I would bolt. They may have been right.

I was getting panicky, now that we were apparently getting ready to move down for arraignment. I was certain I'd be turned loose at once, at least with a minimum bail. But there was the niggling worry of that remark about my name having gone out over the radio. If it was such a phony and trumped-up charge against me, then why the publicity? I wasn't that well-known a literary figure, God knows. So why? And the thought hit me that it might not be such a shoo-in. That my pretty baby face with its day growth of stubble might not be enough to get me out of this jam.

So my buddy's presence might well have been attributed not to my inherent good looks and ingenious nature, but to a sensible realization on his part that I was just unstable enough to break and run if I thought this situation was worse than I'd first thought. My reassurance vanished.

I joined the line of prisoners, and as I saw the cuffs being attached to the others, I whispered to my buddy in plainclothes, "Can I go without?" He gave me a benign smile and shrugged. Then he cuffed me. But he held the other ring himself, rather than attaching me to another felon.

Another felon?

Yes, I had begun to think of myself as one. The innocence till judged guilty did not hold. It was a lovely theory, but wretched practice. No one who goes through the System can consider himself innocent, while being herded and locked up and treated like a foregone conclusion.

I *was* a felon, right then.

Yet my thoughts were not free to dwell on semantics. The line was moving out. Not to the elevator, but through the side door from which my plainclothesman had emerged. Down a side-corridor, and up to a larger, sturdier freight elevator. We waited, and finally the door slammed

155

back. A decrepit old man in grey uniform was operating the machine, and he looked at us as though he had seen a million of us for a million years past. We were fodder for the legal machinery. He was a thoroughly dead old man. I wondered if he was a trusty.

We were loaded into the elevator, and I saw Pooch come on, cuffed to a grizzled veteran of the penal system, busily picking his nose and scratching at his denim shirt.

We went downstairs? Upstairs? I don't even know.

Then began a dizzying series of shunting-abouts, in and out of corridors, pens, cages, enclosures, all of which smelled faintly of vomit, urine and carbolic acid. The smell of a jail is a thing you never forget. There are bitter, acrid and sometimes gagging smell-memories of Lysol, carbolic acid and paraldehyde, a chemical used to quiet drunks, one drop, one-millionth of a drop of which, leaves a scent in the nostrils that never really departs.

And there is the stench of human bodies, of the sweat of guilt and tension. The odor of cosmolene from the guard's guns, and the smell of all-purpose oil used on the locks. The smell of rain-wet coats, and the smell of bad breath. The smell of old leather from cracked shoes, and the smell of absolute desperation.

It is a stink that must offend God, for Man cannot take it for too long, and its persistence in reality *should* offend God. (But after a few hours in the System, one begins to suspect there is no God. If it be true there are no atheists in a foxhole, then it is equally true that there are no true believers in a prison.)

We came out of the labyrinth, through a door, a heavy fire-door with triple locks, passed a little entrance that showed us the outside, still grey and pelted with slimy rain, and we all yearned to go through that entrance ...

But we had been put into the System, and like the Army, once in formation, you were trapped for the duration: Of the day, of the term, of the lifetime ...

All of us—perhaps a third of the number who had been in the larger pen upstairs (downstairs?)—were hustled into a very tiny waiting cell with two benches. The heavy wooden door to the left of the cell opened, and we saw through into the courtroom.

We were there, ready to be arraigned. Ready to find out if we would be free men or temporarily placed in durance vile.

My plainclothesman came up to me at the bars and said, "Do you have a lawyer?" It was the first time the thought had occurred to me. "No," I answered, "I'll plead my own case." It seemed that simple. I was innocent, what did I need a lawyer for . . . wasn't a man innocent till adjudged guilty in this court, as in any court?

He looked worried. "You'd better get a public defender," he advised. "It may be tougher in there than you think."

"You really think so?" I asked.

Näive? Jeezus, Pollyanna move over, here comes Ellison.

"I think you'd better."

He was damned serious, and the cold feeling crept up through my guts to my neck and my face, and I had a sensation of falling. "Would you get him for me?" I asked. He nodded and went out through the wooden door to the courtroom.

In a little while he came back, with me still hanging on the bars like a mounted animal, and he said, "The man's name is Strangways; be here in a minute." I thanked him, and the cop added, "Your mother and Miss Solomon and your agent and some other people are out there. They asked me how you were."

"Tell them I'm fighting mad," I said, sounding anything but.

He grinned, tapped my hand in reassurance, and disappeared again. I turned around to see what was happening in my cell, and that was when all hell broke loose.

CHAPTER THIRTEEN

It was as though someone had said "Roll 'em" and the Marx Brothers had gone into their act. From doors on all sides of the cell, little men with pads of notepaper erupted. Doors slammed. Guards appeared out of nowhere. The prisoners flung themselves against the bars to talk to the little men. The noise level went up a million-fold. It was sheer bedlam. I was grabbed by the scruff of the neck and literally hurled away from the bars, as a brawny derelict moved forward to talk to an approaching note taker. These, apparently, were the public defenders, hauled away from their practices in the awful early morning hours, to try and defend the scum of New York's streets, without fee, without honor, and usually, I was to discover, without success.

Some of them were registered lawyers who devoted a portion of their time—at the Court's "request"—to the defense of those unable to afford counsel. Some of them worked full-time for the Legal Aid Society. Some of them were philanthropists. Most of them were woefully overworked and frighteningly incompetent.

They bounced back and forth from the barred waiting cell to the courtroom, back and forth, here and gone, back and gone again, like the ping-pong balls in the air-vent machines used on TV to show how an air conditioner operates. Most of them were balding, and the image of them ricocheting between "clients" and courtroom would have been ludicrous, had not so many men's very existences depended on their ritualistic gyrations.

I sat down on one of the benches, and tried to read, not really knowing what was happening, nor if one of these budding Clarence Darrows was for me. The noise was deafening, and the phrase most heard, over the din, always tinged with a red frenetic tone, was, "You gotta get me outta this!"

I tried to blot out the noise, but it was impossible. They were like animals, fighting for a piece of meat. They reached through and grabbed at the coats and collars of the lawyers, and those worthies shook them off with slaps and harsh phrases, with wrinkled-up noses and utter contempt. *Are these the men who will speak for us before the bench?* I thought.

They no more wanted to be here, wasting their time on unfortunate bastards without a cent in their pockets, than they wanted to be on our side of the bars. *How doomed we are,* was all I could think, and though it may sound melodramatic, just consider for a moment: the way the System is run today, with all our metropolitan courts so terribly glutted with cases that lawsuits wait a year and two years before they can be heard, with felonies and minor infractions of the law heaped one upon another onto the calendar, with judges overworked and harassed, with a surfeit of poverty and a scarcity of counsels who put the Law before the Dollar...what man has a chance without hired representation?

Consider: you are before a judge who has handled over fifty cases in the past three hours, who is sweltering in his robes, and distressed at the whining voices coming from in front of him; you are unfamiliar with the rules of the game, or you are not glib and fast on your feet; you don't know what to say and even if you did he doesn't want to hear it. If you've been picked up, you must have done what you're accused of having done.

So they send you a public defender, who is totally incapable of helping you, but in whom you put your momentary trust. And he has sixty, seventy, eighty different cases to trot before the magistrate in a matter of minutes. He doesn't know you, has no idea whether you are guilty or innocent, and doesn't really care. It is an obligation; he has been told to do the best he can for you, and so he pumps up to the bars, takes the sketchiest information, and runs back into the court to plead on the arraignment for the poor devil that went before you. Then he rushes back to you, having lost the train of your explanation, makes you start over again, stops you midway with, "Okay, okay, you told me all that ... what I want to know is what your excuse was." He cannot remember what you've said previously, he doesn't give a damn about what you're saying now, all he wants is a few choice words to throw together in some semi-logical order to make a feeble showing before the judge ... a grandstand attempt ... a sham effort ...

"Ellison?"

I sat there, considering the plight of all those poor dumb bastards who wouldn't have a feather's chance in the courtroom, who were going out there to get arraigned and slapped into the Tombs till they met bail or were transferred for trial. I wanted to scream at these phony creeps with their yellow note paper pads, "You're louses, all of you! Nothing but goddam students of the law and you don't care what happens to any of these men! You shouldn't be allowed to practice! These men need help, not play-actors like you!"

"Ellison? Is Ellison in here?"

How terrible it was, to know you were going up against the System, the Machine, the Beast, with nothing standing between you but a paper lance. How terrible to know that the massed indifference and cynicism and boredom of the men of the law were ready to crush you, mold you and force you into a false position, with no help from these bland, dewy-eyed lads who came down to practice on you; like apprentice barbers in a tonsorial school. If you got sliced by their straight razors, or had a chunk taken out of your ear, well, it didn't really matter: Who were you? Just another face. Just another guy with a stubble from having slept overnight in the Charles Street station. So what did it matter.

"Hey! Ellison! Ellison Harlan, Harlan Ellison! Is there someone here named Ellison or Harlan or something like that?"

I suddenly realized that a tall, good-looking man in a Brooks Brothers sport jacket and dark slacks was standing on the other side of the bars, with the animals trying to grab his lapels and his attention, calling for me.

"I'm Ellison, hey, I'm Ellison," I yelled, jumping up.

"C'mere. C'mon, c'mere already, will you. I've got other cases waiting in there, you shouldn't slow me up that wa—"

He never got a chance to finish telling me what a ghastly inconvenience I was to him. A guard poked his head in through the wooden door from the courtroom. "Strangways?" he yelled, and my Defender whirled, belting back, "Yeah, what's happening?" The guard jerked a thumb toward the courtroom, and my Defender, the Right Honorable Upholder Of Speed and Facility, Attorney Strangways, urged me to, "Stay right there. I've got a case up, I'll be right back . . ."

And he was gone.

So help me God, he said: "Stay right there." It sounds like a bad W. C. Fields gag. It sounded that way then. But he said it. He really did.

I couldn't laugh. It was too uncomplicatedly frightening to laugh about.

I went back to sit down and read, and wait for Mr. Strangways to work me into his crowded poor-man schedule.

Pooch was sitting there, staring at his hands.

I sat down beside him. I had to lean in close to make myself heard over the noise of the animal herd.

"What're you in for?" I asked.

"ADW," he replied. He wasn't too hip on talking. I really couldn't blame him. ADW. Assault with a Deadly Weapon. A serious offense. Particularly if he'd been nabbed before and had any kind of a record.

I started to say something, I don't know what, when my man Strangways burst through the door again and motioned me to the bars. I patted Pooch lightly on the arm to let him know I'd be back, and went to my counsel. "Now," he began, as though we had accomplished something on his last trip through, "let me have that again."

"Have *what* again?" I asked.

This was incredible.

He gave me a cold look, as though I was wasting his time. "What happened, what happened, boy! Tell me what your story is."

"My *story*, Counselor, is that I'm innocent. I didn't *do* anything. I was just—"

"Yes, yes," he broke in. "I know. I know you didn't do anything, but what are you in here for?"

I decided I'd better cease my lofty tactics and tell this clown everything I could, in hopes he might retain a bit of it, either in his gray cells or his yellow note pad. "I'm a writer," I began, talking rapidly. "I've done two books on juvenile delinquency. I ran with a kid gang for ten weeks, about five years ago, to gather background data. When I came out of the gang I had a bunch of weapons I used for lectures before PTA groups, youth groups, that sort of thing. A guy I haven't seen in a few years, who wanted to hang me up, called the police and told them I had an arsenal. They picked me up on the Sullivan, and I have a perfectly legitimate use for the weapons—I never *thought* of the gun as a weapon, only as a visual aid, or I would have had the pin pulled and had it registered. Anyway, I've been out of the state for the last few years and I haven't *done* any—"

He broke in rudely, "Ever used it for an illegal purpose?"

"What're you, kidding or something?" I was outraged.

"I just *told* you, I'm a legitimate writer, and I used it when lecturing to youth groups, YMCA classes, that kind of jazz. Don't you believe me?"

"Sure, sure," he indicated no belief whatsoever, putting a palm up to placate me. "I believe you. I'll see what I can do. Wait here." And the Lone Ranger was gone again.

I had a feeling with this bush league Perry Mason on my team I might wind up on the guillotine, rather than in the slammer.

And all the while, the other inmates were clamoring and jostling and going a little mad trying to get heard.

Strangways came rushing through, with a set of briefs under his arm, and I thought he was coming to talk to me, but he called out another name and a seedy old man leaped up from where he'd been sitting cross-legged on the floor, and they huddled (much as I had) for about thirty seconds. Then Strangways bolted again, as a guard held the door for him. (It looked like a *torero* making a pass at the bull, and as Strangways went spinning through the door in his own personal *veronica*, I felt like hollering *Ole!*)

Then I went cold all over, because I was yelling to the vanishing Strangways, and I realized I'd been yelling for almost a full minute, and I heard my voice above the other desperate animals in that pen.

I was yelling, "You gotta get me outta this!"

Then, much later, while my head was spinning so completely from the noise, they let me out of the pen, and it was my turn to go before the arraigning judge. I gave Pooch a feeble look, hoping I'd never see him again in that cell, and watched him mouth the words, "See you soon, man."

The only impression I now have of that few seconds before the bar was a room very heavy with wood paneling, a great many people, the scent of rain-wet clothes, a great deal of bustle and confusion, and half a dozen public de-

163

fenders, bailiffs, cops, guards, hangers-on and crying women, all clustered around the bench.

I had no idea how the judge could see me, examine me, hear my plea. As it turned out, I needn't have worried about it. He never bothered.

Pay attention, then. This is the face of preliminary justice in the morning courts of New York City:

The clerk read off the charge in a monotone, the Judge scratched his white hair, examining himself for signs of dandruff, my Knight In White Button-Down Armor, the sharp and pithy Mr. Strangways, came bursting on the scene and said (so help me God this is word-for-word):

"Your Honor, this man is a writer. He obtained these weapons in the pursuit of a story and he has a legitimate right to own them, becau—"

WHAT DO YOU MEAN HE HAD A RIGHT TO OWN THEM? came the voice of someone's God. SINCE WHEN DOES BEING A WRITER GIVE HIM ANY RIGHT TO OWN A WEAPON? ONE THOUSAND DOLLARS BAIL.

I nearly fainted.

"Your *Honor*," whined Strangways, "five *hun*dred!"

ONE THOUSAND DOLLARS BAIL.

And that was that.

Strangways didn't say another word. He turned on his heel, picked up a new set of briefs on another poor soul, and disappeared into the room with the cage. I stood there, waiting for a chance to say something, but that chance never came. I had had it. Completely.

God, the absolute futility I felt! The helplessness! The need to say or do something! And not being able to move an inch, being so confused by what had happened and its rapidity that I was still lost in a fog!

I turned slowly around as a bailiff grabbed me, and I saw my mother and Linda and my friend Ted White, the jazz critic with his wife Sylvia, and they were absolutely stark white with disbelief and terror. I caught sight of my agent, Theron Raines, and I felt compassion for him, for

164

gentle Theron was practically faint with helplessness at what had happened to me, his friend and his client.

"You got the bail money?" the bailiff asked me.

I don't even know if I answered him.

He dragged me back into the room with the cage, and they tossed me back into the pen with the other losers.

I was down the toilet now. Completely. I had been booked, mugged, printed, and at last, arraigned. It was the end of the game-playing. The Author was now a felon.

Pooch grinned. "Welcome home, man," he said.

All I could think of was that my mother was out there, who knew in what condition. This kind of thing might very well kill her. I can't think of any mother who enjoys seeing her pride and joy being hauled away to the pokey.

I didn't have too much time to think about it, though, for Strangways came trotting back in. "Have you got the bail money?" he asked.

I shrugged. "No, I haven't got that kind of money, but my agent's out there, Mr. Raines—"

"Yes, I met him," he said. "Well, I'm sorry I couldn't do more for you."

I wasn't feeling too salutary at that point. "Thanks anyway," I replied, "If you'd done any more I might have gotten the chair." He looked at me as though I was some kind of a whack, and didn't I appreciate all he'd done for me, taking off from his valuable, money-grubbing, ambulance-chasing practice to come down here to help me— and I was probably guilty anyhow.

All I could think of was how he had whined, actually *whined* in front of the Judge. "Your *Honor*, five *hun*dred!" Jeezus God in Heaven! What a *schmuck!* Pity the guy who had no mother, agent or friends in the circus audience.

He went on to his next customer, and another sterling success jousting with the Beast of the Law.

"How'd'ja do?"

I turned to see Pooch waiting for me. He had been talking to his own Legal Aid man. "About as good as you're going to do," I snapped back. I wasn't feeling charitable, either.

Then his man came for him, and he went out to face the Judge and the Judge's justice. I slumped down on the bench and started to crack up.

Unless you have seen the conveyor-belt justice of an overcrowded New York court, until you have felt the helpless inevitability of not being heard, you don't know what it means to be hung up. The Judge was no better or worse a man than any other; if polled, he would consider himself a fine example of what a magistrate should be. But then, Eichmann probably didn't think of himself as a perverted killer, either. Hitler probably never thought of himself as a maniac. This is the nature of the sickness: not to recognize it. Not to know when you are subverting morality and ethics and common humanity in the name of expediency.

This is the sickness of our times, and the men we put in positions of power, to rule us wisely and with an iron hand. The Judge, harassed, tired, overworked, filled with a deadly cynicism and callousness from years of seeing pleading faces before him, impatient and uncomfortable, perhaps even subconsciously guilty about the shabby job he had been forced to pass off as competent, had found it unnecessary to hear any of the facts in the case, and had intoned, "One thousand dollars bail," without really knowing what he was doing. I felt more pity for him, then, and the anger came later; not too much later, but later nonetheless.

He, too, was trapped.

CHAPTER FOURTEEN

Then began the horrors, as I went through the police-detention routine, while awaiting the arrival (from Lord only knew where!) of my thousand dollar bail money.

The Tombs are very clean, brightly lit, and because of this more frightening than the typical romantic conception of Torquemada's inquisition chambers.

The closed-in feeling, the almost claustrophobic terror of being chivvied, harried, moved wherever they want to move you, in a line with dozens of other men, faceless and without freedom—the entire weight of the building, the city, the law, life—everything weighing down on you ... this is the most terrifying single reality of existence in a jail.

Don't believe it: a grown man *can* cry. Frighten him long enough and hard enough, it'll happen.

Pooch came back as they were unlocking the cell. He had done no better than me, and since his bail was set at two thousand dollars—this was the second arrest for ADW—he was considerably worse off. At least I had people on the outside presumably trying to bail me out.

(I was not to learn until much later that day just how hard they *did* try, and the heartbreaks and personal sacrifice involved, nor how my friends truly came through for me.)

I don't know how conditions run in the other, more permanent, prisons of the New York area—Hart or Rikers Island to name just two—but in the Tombs, the goal is to turn you from a human being into a number, a piece of flesh that will obey, a body that will be *where* they want it, *when* they want it. The total de-humanization of a man. And for some of the unfortunates I saw in the Tombs, this was a short step.

The first batch of us who had been remanded to custody were moved out of the waiting pen, and the men tried to hold back, to stay near the little door to the outside world, so grey and cadaverous with rain. The guards shoved them forward roughly, though not with any real brutality, despite the fact that one old man screamed like a chicken, "Keep your f--kin' hands offen me, hack!"

That was my first occasion to hear the prison slang word for guard used. From that moment on, I thought of them as "hacks" also. After all, wasn't I one of the boys?

We were led out through the fire door and down the twists and cross-corridors of the rabbit-warren that is the Tombs maze. We got in an elevator (perhaps the same one we had been on before) and went down . . . way down. It was like being taken beneath the Earth forever.

When we settled, and were led out of the elevator, we crossed a large open area to another heavy barred door, with a metal fire door arrangement bolted to it, and a thick pane of chicken-wired glass set in the middle. The hack who was leading the caravan banged with his fist on the door, and then rang a bell. After a second another face appeared in the glass, noted who was waiting, yelled something we could not hear through the glass, over his shoulder, and unlocked the door.

We marched into the reception area of the Tombs, where I was to spend the next five or six hours, the worst five or six hours of my life. It was a huge marshalling area, with pens along both walls, and, to our left as we came in, a high-countered desk behind which uniformed hacks were busy arranging records and dossiers, preparing

168

files, typing reports, slamming the drawers of filing cabinets, arguing about undecipherable subjects, and in general making a helluva racket. Down the spine of the room ran two long wooden benches—back-to-back—like the kind they have in railroad waiting rooms or in the principal's office of the high school. At the end of the left-hand bench, at the far end of the room, was a grey-slate-colored counter, behind which two men were busily working. One of them was stuffing possessions into a manila envelope, and the other was getting men to sign something in a huge ledger.

Our line stood there for two or three minutes, and Pooch moved up through the ranks to stand beside me. "I think I know a couple'a these hacks," he confided, with a tinge of youthful pride in his voice.

"Awright, let's go," said the hack who had been leading the procession. He had asked some instructions of the Captain, a chunky man wearing a regulation police cap with badge attached, a black tie (a shade too wide for the current fashion, and a shade too slim for the 40's style), and a white shirt. The Captain had apparently advised him where to put us till he was ready to process us.

The hack shoved one of the men forward, and the man stumbled a step, turned and swung heavily, awkwardly at the guard. "Sonofabitch, you better treat me better'n *that!*" he snarled, as the blow went wide of the mark.

The hack stepped in, ponderous operator though he seemed, with amazing agility, and chopped the prisoner across the top of his chest. The man staggered with the blow, so accurately and heavily was it dealt, and fell back. The hack moved in, his fist balled for a direct clubbing. He drew back, ready to belt the prisoner, but the Captain's voice came from the other side of the line of men, from the counter right near us: "All right, Tooley, that's it. Let him alone. He's drunk."

Tooley back-pedaled and snapped a curt, "Yessir, Cap'n," at his superior. He proceeded to get us into a waiting bullpen. Tooley was an exception among the hacks

169

I saw while in the Tombs. While none of them was charming nor debonair, most were just bored and cynical enough so that if you jumped when they said jump, you had no trouble. There was no actual physical brutality, in the strictest sense of the word, though on several occasions I saw hacks defend themselves from out-of-their-nut winos or psycho cases who wanted out. In those instances, they leveled the quickest club or fist and settled the offender's hash without comment. On several occasions I saw men struck by the hacks in a glancing sense, that is, they didn't move fast enough, or they lipped the guard, or were just generally surly. But since none of the guards carried guns, they tried to keep their hands to themselves as much as possible.

A hack with busy fists could get himself very squashed in a matter of seconds if a crowd of outraged pen-residents decided to gang him. So they only nudge when necessary.

Yet their attitude is the damning condition. They don't see their charges as men. These are so much meat, to be processed in a certain manner, at a certain rate of speed, and when you speak to them, it's almost as though they have to readjust their thinking to comprehend that you are a human being, and not some lower form of life.

I would ascertain that most of the hacks were nice guys in private life; family men who loved baseball games and dogs and old ladies, and who would never think of being anything but gentle outside of this grey room that was a Universe in itself. But in the processing room they were something else. They were far from sadistic (though Tooley, to my mind, was a cat who could do with a little pounding), but they were not quite human either.

It was as though having worked around chained prisoners for so long had rubbed off on them. They were not *of* us, but they were not entirely free of the imprisoned taint, either. It is a peculiar feeling, a strange aura they possess, and I can't explain it any more fully than to say that though they were ostensibly on one side of the Law, and we were on the other, we were very much brothers ...

chained together by what they did to us and what we were forced to *let* them do to us. It is a strong bond, based in hatred, but identifiable with the authority of a father or brother.

There were exceptions, of course.

Tooley, who seemed to be a thoroughgoing bastard who delighted in the kicks he could get by humiliating his prisoners, on the one end of the chain . . . and the Captain, who had given indication of moderation, intelligence and humanity, on the other.

But at that moment we were prey to Tooley, not the Captain, and as we were hustled into the bullpen, I had a feeling that if Tooley could get away with thumbing our eyes behind the Captain's back, he'd do it.

The beefy hack slammed the barred door and locked it. Now began the waiting, till they had processed the bunch of prisoners in the next pen down the line.

I sat down on a hard bench and looked around. The pen was much larger than the one upstairs, but it was the same gun-metal grey color, with a floor that was covered with bits of paper, empty candy wrappers, pools of moisture that might have been urine and might have been anything, with a barred window at the back of the cell (but outside the cell itself) in a little narrow space between the wall of the building and the pen itself. The window was open and the wind was blowing in, and it was damned cold, with the rain slanting through, making it impossible to stand in the rear of the cell without getting wet.

I looked around at my compatriots, and the men therein assembled were as miserable a bunch as I'd ever seen. Not miserable in the social sense of the word, but miserable in the strictest literal sense. They were unhappy men. Tormented men, perhaps. They ranged from the oldest, dirtiest vag with his rose-nose and bloodshot eyes to the youngest Ivy cat all wide-eyed and terrified at being tossed in here with all these *cri-min-als*.

A hack came up to the door and said, "Okay, a couple of you guys clean up them loose papers there." Two of the

171

eager young tots, anxious to seem cooperative, hustled about and cleaned up the floor of scraps. Now the bullpen around me was clean and bare, except for the puddles I now recognized as water that had come in through the open window.

Clean and bare, like my spirit at the moment. Fresh out of platitudes and pithy observations. Pooch sat down next to me. "Crumby buncha shits, ain't they?" he asked.

I shrugged. They were no better or worse than the ones on the outside. The only difference was location.

There wasn't anything else to do, the waiting now having begun, so I talked to Pooch. "So tell me, what's happened to the bunch?"

He gave me a peculiar expression, as though I should have known, and if I didn't where had I been, and come to think of it where *had* I disappeared to, after the big rumble?

"You been away, huh?" he asked, suspiciously.

"Yeah, uh, I moved out of the neighborhood," I parried.

"Y'know," he observed, a bit sluggishly, I thought, "you don't look the same's I saw you last time. You look, I dunno, older or somethin'."

"Well, it's been seven years," I covered.

He nodded acknowledgment, trying to conceive of seven years as time. "Whatcha been doin' with yourself?"

"Oh, you know," I stalled, "the usual. A couple years in the Army, and I got married, and kicking around here and there. You know." That seemed to satisfy him, and he settled back. If he had only known. I was surprised that he hadn't asked me why I'd disappeared after the big fight, but it was a mark of personal integrity in Pooch's set not to ask a man why he had chickened out . . . if that was what he suspected.

"So where's the gang we used to hang around with?" I asked.

He blew air between his pursed lips, puffing his cheeks

like a hamster, and said, "Oh, man, whatta drag. I'm just about the onny one left. They all either split or *got* split."

I urged him to tell me what fate had befallen the tots I'd run with in the Barons, and at first it was as though he was reluctant to talk because they were gone—almost like speaking ill of the dead. But then he started talking, and he told me each kid's story. This is what I learned:

Candle had fallen in love. The boy who had despised Puerto Ricans had fallen in love with a dark-eyed, thin-ankled muchacha, and had not known it. Her name was something very Anglicized, and Candle had met her at a dance. They had started going together, and after three months the girl was pregnant. Her family pounded Candle's name out of her, and one night a three-car caravan had come down from her neighborhood and caught the boy. They had offered him the chance to marry her, but as he stared into their faces, seeing their flat peon look, reflecting his own accursed features, he had spat at them and called them garbage. They had taken him into an alley and beaten him. They did not stop with the bike chains or the boards with nails in them. They went on with a broken bottle, and changed Candle's appearance so completely he would never again have to worry about being mistaken for a Puerto Rican. In fact, he would have difficulty being mistaken for a human being. They cut his right eye so severely that he was blinded, and the muscles of his face went completely limp. They left him for dead and took the girl to a Puerto Rican abortionist who specialized in the love-children of attractive young Latin misses. The girl died on the table. Candle was taken to Bellevue and for what it was worth, they saved his life. He was now living in another neighborhood, somewhere uptown, working as a clerk in a grocery store, and paying periodic visits to an institution to help the handicapped, and a grave in a Harlem cemetery.

Filene had been broken in properly. She had discovered sex as it should be discovered, and had found it was not as frightening as she had believed. After Cheech had disap-

peared (and she had spent Saturday nights cruising 42nd Street, hoping to get a glimpse of him in the pizza joints and flea-bag movies) she took up with Tarzan, who, once he was informed how she liked to be handled, treated her gently and with the utmost art a teen-ager bent on education can employ. She had not allowed Tarzan to burn his initials in her breast, and so when Tarzan contracted a serious case of breaking and entering, she moved on to a new boy in the neighborhood, a blonde boy named Speed, who had come from Pittsburgh and knew all sorts of new ways to dance, and have fun in the bushes. She was arrested for indecent exposure in Central Park with Speed, and though she was not booked, her mother and father beat her severely, and she left home. She took thirty-five dollars from her mother's purse and got as far as she could on a bus. When her money ran out she worked for a time as a waitress in a roadside diner, until she had enough money to get to an Aunt's home in Boise, Idaho. The Aunt tried to send her back, but Filene would not go, and when the family said they did not want her back, the Aunt let Filene live with her. Six months later Filene met a young man who sold health insurance, and they were married the following June. Her picture in bridal veil was run in the social section of The Idaho Statesman. She clipped the picture and sent it to her parents, with the words DROP DEAD scrawled across the face in red marking crayon.

Fish had taken to shooting pool for a living. He got very good at it, and was considered by the sharks in that particular sea a very good man with a "bridge" or "ladies' aid" as they sometimes called it. He ran one hundred and eighteen balls during a certain high-stake game of rotation, and was declared the absolute champ of the neighborhood. When he hit eighteen he enlisted in the United States Army and served eight months at Fort Dix, New Jersey before he was arrested by the C.I.D. for pilfering foot lockers. He was court-martialed, sentenced to six months at hard labor and a dishonorable discharge, which *was invoked at the end of his term in the stockade. He returned to Brooklyn, found most of the gang gone their ways, and cut out cross-country for Las Vegas. He was struck down and killed by a Thunderbird in Salt Lake City, Utah, while fleeing the owner of a Chrysler Imperial who had discovered him trying to jimmy open the door with a coat hanger. He was returned to Brooklyn for burial, an expense his father had to go to HFC to carry off.*

Fat Barky became a bartender in the bar where his father got down on all fours and barked for his booze. He very often gave his father free drinks and paid for them out of his own pocket. Shit managed to get a scholarship to CCNY and became interested in geology. He majored in the subject and graduated with a Bachelor's degree, to find he could not obtain a position with the government Interior Department. He went to work as a floorwalker in a department store. He was still there. Goofball had moved away with her family when they became aware of her alliances with the Barons. No one knew where they had gone. No one cared. Flo became pregnant, no one knew by whom, and managed to extract seventy dollars from nine beaus, each of whom suspected it might be him. She used the money to go to a "rest farm" where the baby was born and sold to a family that could not get a child through normal adoption channels. She drifted back to New York, this time Manhattan, and began a very unspectacular career of getting picked up in bars and selling her body. She was around, as far as anyone knew. Or perhaps they meant she was "round."

Pooch had been unable to grow up. He had been Prez of the Barons for too long. It was his glory, his only status, and he needed it as badly as a lush needed his juice. When the contemporaries began drifting away, and the junior

175

gang members began growing up into his place, Pooch was forced out by democratic vote, and took to hanging around the streets. He managed to get picked up for attacking a garage owner with a switch-blade, and served six months in Bellevue Detention Home. When he was released he tried to enlist in the Marines, but they would not take him because of his record as a delinquent. He tried the other services and was treated the same. Belligerent, he started robbing candy stores, toy stores, pharmacies, garages, private homes, getting what he could, whether it was worth fencing or not. He was arrested for breaking and entering, petty larceny and resisting arrest, and served one year on Rikers Island. When he got out he tried to get a job, found himself hanging around the streets with the same kids he had known as junior Baron recruits, and when pushed by his parole officer to get straight or go back to the Island to finish his sentence, attacked the man with a fireplace poker. He was arrested for ADW and found himself back in the Tombs, sitting beside a guy he had not seen in seven years.

I listened to all the stories of the kids I had known, and the view was a terrible one. They had gone the way they had started. The seeds of rot had been planted so early, and they had ripened to produce diseased fruit. Every one of them . . . every one in some way inadequate or hostile or scared or corrupt. And I wondered, then, how much I could have done for them. I wondered if I'd failed them as much as I thought I had. Could I have done anything to save them, to turn them away from the dead ends?

I didn't know, and my heart ached in me as I thought of all of them; the ones I'd liked and the ones I'd hated, and the ones I'd even loved in a way. And it seemed that I was more guilty than any society that had done this to them. I was more guilty than the teachers who had not taught them, and the clergymen who had not given them faith, and the parents who had ignored and corrupted them. I was more guilty than all of them, because I *knew* and I had run away to write about it.

To keep my hands clean.

To play the dilettante.

I had refused to pay my dues.

And now I sat here beside Pooch, seven years later, and I was a big-deal pillar of the community, and he was a gutter urchin, and neither of us was better than the other.

We were both in Hell.

CHAPTER FIFTEEN

The bullpen around me was clean and bare, and filled with the naked faces of men who were guilty, except for the innocence in their hands . . .

Here it was, all laid out for me, full circle and with whatever meanings I felt like charging to my scene. I knew there would be men who had spent longer in jail than I had, who would scoff at what I was thinking, saying, "What the hell are *you* making such a big thing for? You haven't been in long. You ought to try it for ten years or so. *Then* you can play the martyr." I knew there would be people who would say I was making a big social *megillah*, a federal case, a mountain out of a molehill, from my one lousy day in the slammer. Guys who would call me a bleeding heart, and a fanatic, and a kook, because I saw what I'd seen and interpreted it the way I had. People who would say, "Hell, I've been in the can, too, and I just laughed it off. You're making a big case out of a little problem." And they might be right. Perhaps I should have taken it easy and settled back and waited for the bail to come through—as I knew it had to, eventually. Perhaps I shouldn't have beaten my chest and pissed and moaned about the Inglorious Evils Of A Corrupt System. Perhaps I should have played the clown, as would these others, with ribald little tales of my goofy, happy-go-lucky sojourn in the pokey.

But that wasn't the way it was for me.

It wasn't a game or a lark or something to laugh at.

It was a place where men are sent to pay for their sins ... that's the strictest literal purpose of a prison, you know ... where you can smell the stink of desperation, and the odor of men's souls slowly rotting. I saw it in those terms, and to write about it any other way would be selling out.

It is possible to be petty and literarily inventive and caustic and bored by this sort of scene, and I presume that is what is considered sophisticated and very hip. But don't talk of sophistication or hipness to a vag full of rotten, sour liquor and crab lice. Don't talk about the chic of being a jailbird to a seventeen-year-old kid locked in a cell with case-hardened homosexuals, junkies in the first stages of withdrawal, acknowledged rapists and heist artists, deadbeats and homicidal types. Don't tell me about how I could take it with a twinkle and a chuckle and away we go, because that's a pile of pseudo-sophisticated horse manure! It all comes down one way, and that way is pure and simple and don't give me any of your sophistic guff about being too serious when a smile will help.

I *know* it stinks in the Tombs.

I *know* I saw young cats being warped and altered and twisted right in front of me.

So get away from me with that crap. This is the way it *is*, not the Pollyanna pink lace and rose-colored glasses tomfoolery we use in this country to delude ourselves about everything from True Love to Disarmament. We are going straight to hell, gentle reader, and if you need proof of it just get yourself pinched in New York, or go out in the streets and dig those kids.

And somehow, without meaning to do it, I've made the point of this book ... even before I've finished writing it. I've made what desperate little point I have to make, and all the rest is anti-climax. We're in trouble. We're in serious trouble. It's like Jim Baldwin says, the only way we'll solve—for instance—"The Negro Problem" is if we solve The American Problem. So don't look for hidden meanings and morals, friend, I'm not subtle enough to give them to you candy-coated. The word is simply that for all our national pride and all our jingoism and all our heavy-duty platitudes, this country is losing a lot of battles, and we are sitting around with our fingers up our noses deluding ourselves that we're doing just fine, thanks, just fine.

It all ties in. It's all part of the scene. It's Purgatory, with singing commercials. Hell with an 8-cylinder fish-finned Detroitmobile. It's Perdition with indoor plumbing.

And it's a teen-aged kid named Pooch locked away in a cell with forty other damned souls, waiting to find out if he's going to spend some years of his life behind walls too high to climb, or be turned back into the streets, to do the best he can until his luck runs short.

That's why I wrote this book.

That's why I knew I'd write it, in that bullpen.

And when this book is done, I'll shut my mouth.

It was something out of Kafka or Dinesen, almost surrealistic, the narrow grey world of the bars; dark and many-faceted, and constantly terrifying. I saw two Negro homosexuals sitting close together at one end of a bench, almost hugging each other. They were a fine pair of spokesmen for their people. They were junkies.

I asked myself, who did this to them? Did they do it to themselves, with weak characters? Or did the ofay, the White Man, do it to them, with his "culture"? And I didn't have an answer. But it seemed to me that they were more offensive a millionfold than White fags would have been. Because here was a race that was on the move, on the march, as Baldwin—again—put it, "The Magic People." It was true, and these two men, correction: individuals, were no part of it.

They huddled together like a pair of small, thin girls, their Continental slacks so tight they fit like leotards, and so short I could see the bad taste of their striped socks. One was in bad shape. He needed a fix and he was going to need it even worse, very shortly. He was bone-sick then, and he sat with his right leg crossed over his left so completely that his right foot wound around back of his left calf and hooked around the shin. He had his arms folded across his stomach as though someone had slit him up the middle and he was afraid his cold guts would drop out unless he held them in. That one was the old queer, a cruising queen who had turned too many other young cats on to be left in circulation. His partner was a pretty, very hairy swinger whose clothes reeked with inbred filth, but who smelled lovely from the perfume daubed behind his ears. And I thought of these lovers: *You stink, Group. You really stink. No one condemns you for your morals, or your odor, or your habit, or your skin color. They condemn you because you show how rotten a good thing can get when there's no personal integrity, when there's no character.*

They weren't even niggers. They *certainly* weren't Negro, despite the color of their skins. They were something almost sub-human, on the way out, and hanging on, doing harm, by creating an image.

Their sin was their existence.

Next to them was an old man, his clothes of fairly good grade and his weathered, pocked face clean-shaved, still red and puffy from scraping too close with a straight razor. He was shaking. Terribly. Convulsively. As though his clockwork mechanism was beginning to shudder to a stop.

Even as Pooch and I watched him, he leaped up and threw himself staggeringly against the barred front of the cell, and the door sprang open ...

I had thought it had been locked, but apparently they were planning to move us down the induction line, and had left it unlocked.

He went bursting through, arms flailing like a great blue serge seagull, his collar points upthrust and white, his hair like blowing snow showers, his eyes quite mad, and his mouth agape. He flung himself into the compound, and the hacks were on him in a moment, trying to pin him, trying to silence his screams, trying to avoid the other men's going berserk. But the old man, the poor old man who wanted his taste of rotgut and was quite out of his head, would not be silenced. He flung himself about, over the benches, across the floor, banging his feathery head against the steel barred doors.

And finally Tooley, our friend with the teeth Tooley, the hack Tooley, caught him with a shoe-tip. He caught the old man in the gut, and the old man rolled over gasping, like a beached fish. The guards picked him up, and I heard the Captain say something about violent ward and Bellevue. And then the old man was gone.

All he'd wanted was his juice.

I never felt like crying so hard for someone I'd never known. But he was gone, and I was still here, and Pooch was withdrawing into himself, and I wanted to tell him who I was, really, and what I was doing here, and what I'd been doing in the Barons. But it wouldn't have worked.

Communication is a strange thing.

When you need it most, it fails.

"Awright, you prisoners," a hack yelled, coming up to the still open door of the bullpen, "we got cake'n coffee an' a few sanniches here for ya, so file out one atta time an' take one helping is all." A trusty in grey wheeled up a huge stainless steel serving cart.

I didn't feel like eating. My stomach was numb.

All around me the noises of the bullpen, strange and in their own way jungle-like, merged together to make one great clamor. The men dashing for the food outside the cell, the coughs, the mumbled dirty words, the hissing sound of men with unruly systems breaking wind, the snoring of a lush sleeping it off before they roused him, the tinny whine of cowards' voices and the brassy boom of braggarts back for their fiftieth journey. It was all the same, as Pooch came back and sat down, a brown-bread sandwich of butter (oleo?) and a tin cup of watery black coffee in his hands.

"Whyncha go and get something?" he asked.

I shook my head. "Not hungry."

"Good coffee," he mumbled, sipping at the steaming thin stuff.

I figured the coffee might help. I walked out and drew a cup with the ladle. One of the prisoners standing just inside the door hissed at me, then urged, "Take a sandwich."

"No, thanks," I said, dumbly.

"Take a sandwich; you sonofabitch, *take* a sandwich!"

I walked back into the cell, and he stepped in front of me. "What the fuck's the matter with you, you dumb bastard? *Take a sandwich!*"

"Say, what the hell is your problem?" I jammed him. He was a big, nasty-looking cat, with two sandwiches and two cups of coffee, one in his hand, the other propped against the wall on top of the metal partition shielding the toilet. "I'm not hungry, I don't *want* a sandwich," I concluded. I tried to elbow past, but he stopped me roughly, and shoved me back with his hip.

"For me, you little c—"

I didn't need to have him outline it in Anglo-Saxon. I went back and drew him another sandwich. I hoped he'd choke.

We sat there, Pooch and me, and I had nothing to say. I was feeling miserable. Lonesome and sad and just plain gritty. Then a hack came up to the cell and yelled, "Throw your extra food inna disposal can there, and line up out here." The vags who hadn't eaten since hitting the slammer the night before weren't about to waste the food, so they stuffed it in their mouths and fell into line.

Aside from the two queers, most of the men were Negroes, hauled in for a number of charges from wife-beating and knife-fighting to policy and numbers raps, possession of narcotics (or "holding" as we cons called it), non-support, exposing their privates in public, drunk &

183

disorderly, assault, disturbing the peace, authentic auto theft and simulated rape.

They were, however, the cleanest-looking of the prisoners, and carried themselves with more dignity than their ofay brothers, who were here for aggravated assault, pushing junk, prostitution, gambling, auto theft (in this case known as "boosting"), confidence robbery, grand larceny, failure to pay traffic fines, authentic rape and simulated murder.

My hammer-killer was nowhere to be seen.

But he had been replaced by the Sandwich-Gobbler, who looked like something out of Long John Silver's nightmares. He was as swarthy and beefy and nasty looking a cat as I've ever seen, and while I suspected him of the foulest deeds known to Western Man, I'm sure he was in for something innocuous, like poisoning pigeons in Washington Square.

"Beat it," I heard Pooch say, with a snarl, and turned around to look at him behind me.

One of the fags, the younger one, the Princess, had propositioned him. Great fun for a Monday outing.

The line moved out, turned left, and we passed in front of the wooden counter.

I figured now was my time to make my play.

"Hey, I want to call my lawyer," I said.

"No phone calls," I was told.

"But—"

"No phone calls. You can write a message on this form," the hack said, passing me a 5 x 8½ sheet on which I could list my name, offense, and message. I stepped aside, borrowed a pencil (which bugged the ass off the hack) and wrote a note to my agent, Theron. It said, simply:

PLEASE GET THE BAIL MONEY AND GET ME OUT OF HERE PLEASE! IF YOU DON'T GET IT SOON AND COME FOR ME, THERE WON'T BE ANY NEED TO BOTHER. PLEASE!

I gave the note to the hack, he read it, laughed, and

shoved it into a little box. Lord only knew how long I'd wait before that note got to the proper party.

I got back in line, behind the younger fag, watching my rear at all times, for the older one, the junkie, still clutching himself, was behind me.

"Take everything out of your pockets," I was listening to the hack behind the ledger talking to the young fag.

The young queen lisped (so help me!) something quaint and stripped his pockets clean. I thought it was lovely that he had carried two bottles of his favorite scent with him, as well as a bottle of new, clear Stopette roll-on deodorant.

Then it was my turn. They took everything, including my money and my glasses, tossed them all into a manila envelope, and passed me down the line into a disrobing room where everyone was undressing, putting their clothes into a wire basket provided by a hack.

I heard one of the young guys who had been in line ahead of me squeal as the fag struck again. I cursed inwardly, and felt myself reeling just a bit. What a madhouse!

The hack in attendance went through everybody's clothes in the baskets, slapping the shoes hard to make sure there were no files, knives, packets of heroin or razor blades in the heels or soles. He turned all the jackets and shirts inside out. When he'd done with mine, I offered him my tie to search for a Thompson sub-machine gun, but he didn't think that was funny.

I went into the shower, leaving my basket on the bench in front of the long line of steaming nozzles. It was an education, watching the teen-agers duck and blanch as the fags tried to goose them, studying the scummy bodies of the old men, with their filthy, rotting feet; it was a scene out of Hogarth's *Bedlam*, with the junkies and their scabrous, gray-fleshed arms full of needle tracks, the winos puking on the floor, the lice-ridden derelicts and the masturbators who didn't care *who* watched them as they took their momentary pleasures under the stinging spray of the showers.

I could feel myself slipping again.

One cat got led away to be de-loused. He needed it. He left a vapor trail as he passed. Then I was washed, and stepped forward, to hear a hack yell, "Okay, step over here before you get dressed, over here, over here, c'mon!"

I stepped forward, continuing the dehumanizing but sanitizing assembly line routine, with the Tombs physician waiting to ask how I felt. I might tell him, too.

CHAPTER SIXTEEN

He asked me how I felt, and I said, "Glorious. A delightful little resort you have down here." A hand came out of the right hand portion of nowhere and Tooley slapped me across the side of the head. I told the Doctor I felt fine. He made me spread my toes to show him if I had Athlete's Foot. I said, "Dermatophytosis," and he looked up, shocked that one of his charges would be literate. If he'd known I'd memorized the word off a bottle of foot powder, he wouldn't have been so impressed.

He nudged me ahead with a nod of his head, I went back and got my basket, re-dressed, and walked out of the shower room into another tiny waiting area where they had a fingerprinting set-up ready. They printed me again, and again offered no means of washing the black, condemning stains off my fingers. It was a perfect illustration to me of how they systematically reduce you to an animal. Instead of having the inking ready at the other end of the shower, enabling a man to wash himself clean in the hot water, they wait till he is clean and again bears some vestige of personality, humanity, dignity, and then they rub his nose in his own shit again.

As I stood there waiting to be told what to do next, an old saucehound staggered out of the shower, perspiring terribly from either a disease Herr Doktor Quack-Quack had decided was unimportant, or from the heat of the shower room. He vomited on my shoes, though I leaped back quickly.

The smell remained on my shoes for three days no matter how hard I was to scrub them. I finally threw them away. The memories were bad enough, without olfactory additions.

I stared at my black fingertips with morbid curiosity. A physical reminder that I was a criminal.

It seemed, at that point, that I had been locked away for months. Time has a peculiar and hideous manner in jail. It does not move. It stops completely, and since they have taken away all watches, since there are no clocks in sight, since the hacks will not tell you what time it is, the mind boggles, and you lose sight of the time-flow, and consequently, a little more of reality is stolen away from you, while you feel your mind decaying underground.

The men were being printed and harangued into a cell midway down the line, directly opposite the big bullpen in which the old man had gone berserk. It was a waiting cell, the last one before they transferred you to a home in the main cell blocks.

I knew if they got me in there I'd snap completely. I had to make a move now, or go with the rest of them, get locked away in the Tombs and they'd lose my card and when the bail money came they wouldn't know where I was and I'd become just another person in a cell and they'd tell my mother and my agent and my friends that I must be somewhere else because I wasn't listed here as being in a cell and they would go away and the bail money would lie waiting and I'd be in the Tombs forever and forever and forev—

I caught myself.

That was how it happened, I guessed.

You never know you're a coward until it happens. No. You never know your character is weak until it snaps. You never know how thin the tensile cord of your sanity can be until it breaks. I would have cried, right then, sat

188

down on the floor and wept, I was so scared and lost and lonely and desperate to get *OUT!*

Out!

OUT! I didn't care how, just get me OUT OF HERE!

Pooch was coming out of the shower room as I made my move. All the other men were being put into the temporary cell, till they could be taken away to their regular residences, when I stalked past the hack who was locking them up. I walked past him, and he turned around to say something to me, and I just gave him a peremptory wave with my hand and mumbled something about having the Captain's permission and blah blah blah. He stared at me for a second, but since he knew I couldn't get out of that processing room, and since I was striding toward the front desk and the Captain bent over his papers—as though I actually knew where I was going and what I was doing—he assumed I had been ordered to the desk, and he let me go.

I had perhaps forty feet to cross before I could get to the Captain (and even then I had no idea what I would say to the man), when I saw Tooley coming after me. *He* knew I wasn't supposed to be out of that line.

"Hey! Hey, you, c'mon back here!"

I stopped dead in my tracks. He came up behind me and I'll never forget the feeling of that meathook on my collar as big Tooley literally grabbed me off the floor. He swung me around as though I was a sack of meal, and propelled me before him, back to the cell, midway in the line. He snapped his fingers and the hack opened the cell door, and Tooley cuffed me alongside the head as he booted me forward with his foot. "Now getcha ass in there, and don't try nothin' again or I'll give you a *real* kickina ass!"

Tooley, wherever you are today, know this:

I wanted to injure you. I wanted to hurt you. Every boot in the ass I'd ever gotten, since I was a kid, every cuff in the ear I'd ever taken, since I was old enough to recognize pain, every hurt and every confinement and every inability to strike back was caught up in my fist then,

189

Tooley. You are a fat, sadistic sonofabitch, Officer Tooley. You are the reason so many guys try to break out of jail. You are the reason in this culture for violence and striking back and murder. You are everything lousy and egotistical and crummy, Tooley. And when you gave me that kick in the slats I felt every anti-Semitic bastard who'd kicked me when I was in grade school, and I felt every warped Sergeant in the Army who got his jollies booting troopers around, and I felt every snotty cop who uses his badge to vent his spleen . . . and right then, Tooley, you were close to having me on you. You'd have gone to your grave with my teeth embedded in your throat, Tooley, you rotten sonofabitch!

But . . .

I went flailing across the cell, impelled by Tooley's foot, and brought up short against the opposite wall. I hit it and went sliding, landing in a heap, my raincoat wrapped around my legs. One of the winos helped me up. Tooley had walked away already. The cell was locked. I was trapped again. It was a hopeless cycle. There was no way out.

I was still filled with thoughts of violence toward big Tooley, fat Tooley, sonofabitch Tooley. I tried to be rational about it, tried to tell myself *Hell, take it easy, he's just doing his job. Don't take out all the bitterness you've ever known on him.* Was I speaking for myself, or was I projecting Tooley's kick in the ass as the hob-nailed boot of authority on the neck of every poor slob in the world?

And I knew at once that I was speaking only for myself, but that there was truth in what I'd thought. It *was* men like Tooley who corrupted, men like Tooley hidden behind a badge or a diploma or a white collar whose personalities came before the responsibilities of their position. *Aw, hell,* I said to myself, *you're just bitter. Everybody gets booted around in a lifetime.*

Which was true, of course. But it didn't make me feel any better. I still wanted to kill that mother—!

Rationality is the first thing to go.

I slumped down on the bench, beside the big can full of crap and wet stuff, and my head fell into my hands. It had been a hard day, and there didn't seem to be any end to it. I felt a hand on my arm. I looked sidewise and it was Pooch. "Hey, man," he was speaking very softly, a tone I'd never heard him use, one of real compassion, "what's shakin'?"

I grinned up at him. He made it easier.

"Nothin' shakin' but the leaves on the trees," I replied.

I could see them marching in a new batch of men, across the room, into the cell we'd first occupied, when the old man had flipped and streaked away. They were a bunch very similar to our group (I'd already established rapport with my confined compatriots; it was "our" group).

It was more of the grimy group I'd shared the big cell upstairs with, waiting to go to court. I saw my pal the hammer-killer in the ranks, trotting alongside a kid who couldn't have been more than seventeen or eighteen; every once in a while the kid would look up from under guarded eyes at his traveling companion. That kid was out of his nut with fright. *That* was the crime of the Tombs, right there, all neatly packaged for anyone who wanted to look at it.

The hack unlocked the door, left it standing ajar, and walked back toward the printing bench, instructing a group of men which cell to enter when they'd been blacked on the hands. I said to Pooch, "I'll see you, man, stay cool," and before he could ask me where I was going, I was off the bench, out of the cell and crossing that fifty feet from the cell, past the spot where Tooley had caught me, and right up to the Captain behind the counter.

I started talking, and I talked faster than I ever had before, in a life singularly noted for fast talking and rapidly-employed angles. I'm not sure what I said, but it was something like:

"Captain my name's Harlan Ellison, Ellison, I'm expect-

191

ing my agent and my mother and some friends to get my bail money and get it down here fast in a very few minutes just a little while and honestogod I can't stand being in that cell I've got claustrophobia and if I stay in that damned cell another minute I'll flip and the money'll be here in a few minutes in fact you may have the papers for my release now and if you'll let me sit out here on this bench I swear to God I won't be any trouble and you won't have to worry about looking for me when they come with the papers so why don't you blah and blah and blah . . ."

Either my innocent, ingenuous expression won him, or my babble wore him down, or he knew I was going to be released soon, because he raised both hands to his ears and shook them gently, as if to say all right, all right, you can sit on the bench, just *shut up* and let me get back to work.

He pointed to the end of the bench and said, "Go ahead." I made for that bench as though it were a raft in a stormy sea. I sat right on the edge of it, and at the very end of it, so no one could confuse me with a prisoner about to go into a cell.

Tooley came past, right about then, and took one look at my white, terrified kisser, and made a move toward me. I stopped him fast by gibbering: "The *Captain* said I could sit here the *Captain* the *Captain!* Ask the *Captain!*"

He walked up to the Captain and spoke to him in a low tone for a moment. The Captain said something short and brusque, and Tooley noodled it out and said something else and the Captain dismissed him peremptorily. Tooley walked away, giving me a hateful stare.

I was home free, for a while, anyhow.

Time does not move in jail. That is one of the most overwhelming truths I realized. It does not crawl, it does not slither, it does not budge. There are no watches, no clocks, no ways to tell the passage of the minutes, and no guard will tell you if you ask him. So you have no way of knowing whether it is high noon, three and tea time, five just before dinner, or eight o'clock with darkness on its way. The time-sense becomes atrophied quickly, under the ground, in the Tombs. One finds himself dozing, only to awaken a moment later with the impression three or four hours have passed. After the first few hours, in which the novelty of being shunted about here and there has worn off, I began to feel that I had been down in the cells for a week, not just a few hours. Subjectively, I spent much longer than twenty-four hours in jail . . . it was more like twenty-four months.

And more than any other effect, this pale, trembling timelessness, this experience out of time and space, leaves a person feeling disembodied, prey to any physical ill that happens along, prey to weird schemes and images of the mind. I can see why men go "stir-crazy" in a short time; to them, it's a long time.

While I sat there, disembodied and expectant, breathing once out of every three times (I imagined), another line of men was brought in.

Now that I had nothing to do but sit and stare, I examined them closely. Minutely. These were the vags, the bums, the wineheads and the wetbrains from the Bowery, the Sneaky Pete drinkers and the Sweet Lucy lovers, the ones who filtered bottles of after-shave lotion down through a loaf of pumpernickel, the ones who drank canned heat and panther sweat, the ones who had left too many pieces of themselves in too many bars for too many years. These were even lower than the felons and the thieves and the boost artists. These were the absolute dregs of humanity. Men to whom life had lost its meaning, thought had lost its verve, existence had lost its color. Men with newspaper serving as soles for their shoes, with ragged clothes and ragged faces, with dull eyes and runny noses, with unshaved jowls and uncut hair. Faceless men, into the wrinkles of whose cheeks had been weather-ground the dirt and grit and soot and degradation of half-lifetimes spent on knees, in gutters, in doorways and alleys. These were the men the society had dumped out its backside.

These were the men *they* spoke about when *they* asked: "Are we fulfilling our obligations to our citizens?"

No good to say they could work if they wanted to work. No good to say they were lazy, dirty, stupid, unable to keep a job, irresponsible, shiftless, belligerent. No good.

These were the men who had passed through the mill of our culture, been unable to fit any molds, been unable or unwilling to discover themselves, and been flushed out the rear end of the System. Here was the dung we called the deadbeats.

In the Tombs they are called the "skids."

See them, then. See the truly lost ones. How easy it is to condemn them, when you pass them lying in an alcove, the stench of sour rye on them, their clothes fouled with their own waste. How bloody easy it is to laugh at them and let the kids mug and roll them and cast them out. And the fury of it all is that the outer darkness into which they cast themselves is so much more terrible, so much more final than any social darkness *we* could use.

All of this went through my mind as they stopped right beside my bench. I was close enough to touch four of them—but I didn't.

Old men, they were. Even the young ones. Old men, very tanned, even in September. Tanned from spending their days in the park, in the sun. Old men, their pants baggy and their hair white and their jowls stippled ... almost a dirty uniform. Vests and pin-striped suits with wide, wide lapels, gifts of the benevolent and pretentious, doles from a too-busy citizenry. And the shoes ... the rotting, falling-apart shoes, with the friction tape wrapped around the toes to keep sole and leather together. The rags for stuffing.

And their pallor. Their white, blue-veined, bulbous red pallor that comes right through the tanned, leathery skin. Brown on the surface, and so horribly, fish-belly white underneath. Sick old men, lost old men, decent and starving and frightened old men turned off by luck, turned off by time, turned off by life. Gone to ground, finally, in the Tombs.

For a big Thirty w/3-a-day.

The stench of dead whiskey was almost too pervasive an odor to bear. But I could not move, and would not move, and let them stare at me with their dead, unfeeling eyes, with the sparks gone and just anyoldthing there.

It sounds strange, now, to say it, but I think the most honest emotion I've ever had was while staring at those poor saucehounds and winos. *I wanted to say something to them.* I wanted to tell them they could have a piece of *my* life, if it would help end their misery. Anything to stop the hopelessness of what they had become. They looked back at me without curiosity, seeing a young guy with the world by the tail, and their world was not my world.

They had been lost for a very long time.

And all the good wishes or self-conscious duty-shirkers could not find them. The work should have been done many years before.

A hack, standing nearby, snapped a half-inch cigarette butt onto the floor near the line of vags, and four of them dove for it; the one who came up with it was shaking so badly he burned his lips getting it re-lit for one puff before his spastic movements confounded him.

The lank hair. The unshaved faces. The twitches and starts and odors and shiftings of feet. The very smell of death about them. And the absence of desperation. These men had long since forgotten what desperation was.

Watching them, feeling the humanity draining out of me as the full import of what these ex-human beings had been turned into rose in me, I felt more trapped than ever before by the System.

Because *this* was the reward you got for screwing-up in the Glorious System. This was the ax that fell. And here was a manifestation of the lost, who seemed to be the guilty.

The waiting. The nothing-to-do. The putting my hands before me so I could see the black stains. (And then it dawned on me, why I had been constantly putting my hands through the bars while in a cell. Why everyone did it. Putting my hands through the bars so just a little of me could be free.) The feeling I was no longer a human being. The absolute loss of all humanity. The penultimate agony of realizing my life was in someone else's hands completely, subject to his whim or fancy.

And I couldn't yell: "The game is off. I don't want to play any more!"

It's *their* game, *their* rules.

"Okay, Ellison, let's go."

I stared at the old men, and inside somewhere I honest to God cried for them. They were me, I was them, we were all brothers, and they were down here for keeps.

"C'mon, Author, let's get goin', your bail came through."

Tooley lifted me off the bench, cleared me with the Captain, and hustled me out of the Processing Room, taking me upstairs to be turned loose at last.

I was free.

But I didn't realize it till I was in the reception room. Because the last thing I had seen was all I could still see, all I could remember, what I'd never forget.

The old men.

The ones who could be anyone, who could be me, if I ever lost the drive to keep living, if I ever let the System and Life in all its Mechanized Modern Majesty grind me into the ground.

The old men, and the young men, and the fags, and the winos, and the junkies, and the poor sonofabitch whose life had somehow been warped about the time he should have had his first woman, who had wound up using a hammer on a chick. The old man who needed his juice and wound up with a broken head. The teen-ager who was scared and Tooley who was just crummy. All of them were back down there, like creatures without souls, waiting to see and be seen.

Waiting down there in Hell, in Purgatory, in the Tombs.

Yeah, I was out. I was free. But who would cry for the old men?

CONCLUSION

There are some loose ends to these two periods in my
life. They aren't as important, perhaps, as the stories the
truth tells in what happened to me—among the young
men and among the old men. But they tie everything up in
the accepted non-Existentialist manner we've grown accustomed to expect from Western storytellers . . .

My mother was waiting in the check-out room of the
110 Centre Street building, when they brought me up
from below. She was soaked to the skin, and I realized
that it was still raining. I had a strange feeling that in all
the months I had spent downstairs in the Tombs it should
have stopped raining. A rain that long would have meant
another Noah and his Ark. Then, of course, I realized I
had only been down there one day, just twenty-four hours.
Yet it had seemed so much longer.

My mother told me how she had heard the Judge say
one thousand dollars, and how Linda and Ted White and
my agent Theron had all jumped—almost as one—to say
they would pool their money and buy me a bail bond at
one of the *schlock* bondsmen in the neighborhood. She
told me how she had said she would take care of it, that I
was her son and it was her responsibility, and how they
had all argued to get me out as quickly as possible.

Serita Ellison, my mother, is in many ways a very re-
markable woman. She has great personal strength. A

woman who seems able to stare the most deliberately evil forces of Nature in the eye and not flinch. This is something it took me many years to realize; for her reserve of energy is too often hidden beneath a guise of feminine softness. Yet I have seen her perform acts of incredible stamina for a woman her age, that I would not expect from a person fifteen years her junior. I say this now, for the first time within the reach of her attention, not only as a thank you and a recognition of her importance in my life—a life that many times might have gone very wrong had she not been handy, but as an admission to myself that no one—not even myself, though I'd like to believe it sometimes—is ever *really* alone.

She went out in the storm and she called a money-source I had never even suspected she knew. She called on a man whose name she will not tell me to this day, and she asked him for one thousand dollars. She went up to the lower Forties on the West Side, got the money, and came back, to get me out of the Tombs.

They gave her the usual machine-made runaround.

"Not this building. Take bail money to the other building."

"Yes, we'll take the bail money here, but we haven't gotten the papers on him yet. You'll have to go see the Prosecutor's office."

"No, we don't have the papers here. They went down half an hour ago. Those people are nuts down there."

"Oh, yeah, hey here they are. But we're going out to lunch now. Come back after one o'clock."

"You here again? No, nothing we can do till they get back from lunch. Sorry."

"Yes. We'll have him up in a minute."

And *four hours later,* from the time she presented the money, till the time I was brought through the grilled cage door, she waited in the check-out room, watching a Puerto Rican woman thrash and scream and plead for her own husband to be turned loose; identifying with this

198

woman who spoke no English and was paralyzed with hysteria and fear in the presence of the Machine System.

Four hours, wet and cold and very much afraid this time her kid had done himself in properly. Then I came out, and it was all right again. Everything was all right again.

I got my belongings back from the clerk, and we went back to 95 Christopher Street. As we walked into the building, Jerry, the doorman I had told I was going away on business, the one I had asked to tell my mother to get in touch with Linda Solomon, was standing in the lobby.

Jerry has a ratty way about him, and he could barely contain his enthusiasm as he trotted across the lobby to tell me, "Say, I read about you in the paper this morning ... heard it over the radio, too."

"Heard what, Jerry?" I asked him, already cold with intuitive certainty that *he* had tipped the papers.

"Well, you know, about the trouble with the narcotics and goin' to jail. I mean, you're a tenant here and I recognized the address they gave inna paper."

"Got a copy of that, Jerry?"

He fished around in his wallet till he came up with a scrap of newsprint. It was from the *New York Daily News* and it was headed up by AP—Associated Press. That meant it had gone out over the wires of the AP on Monday morning, September 12th, and every paper in the country would get it. No matter how few picked it up, everyone who knew me, anyone who had read my books and remembered the name of the author, my family (who had been kept in the dark about this by my mother), my publishers, everyone in the trade ... they would all know.

The story was short, but cleverly worded so that (1) it was made clear no narcotics were found, (2) explained that the weapons in question were in my possession for a thoroughly rational reason, and (3) defamed me completely. By inference. By non-statement. Sins of omission. By veiled innuendo. The twisted word, the unstated obvi-

199

ous, the malleable semantic wonder of "Have you stopped beating your wife?"

I gave it back to him, and didn't say anything. I was too hung up to bother taking him apart. Jerry was operating as a stringer for the newspapers. It was common practice; too many bellboys, doormen, elevator operators, desk clerks and cabbies in the city were stringers. For a couple of bucks they'd feed any tip they got in to the City Desk.

Jerry had tipped the newspapers.

It was obvious no one else could have known, since the narcotics charge had died with the two plainclothesmen who had arrested me, and had not even been the booking charge at the Charles Street station. I knew neither of the plainclothesmen had passed it to the tabloids, and I knew the Captain who had finally had me booked at Charles Street would not mention it; so the information had to emanate from somewhere prior to my arrest. Ergo, Jerry, who had been met—apparently—by the plainclothesmen when they had first come looking for me the day before. They had probably identified themselves as being on the Narcotics Squad, found out whether I was in, and come upstairs. When Jerry had seen the three of us go out, he had gotten on the horn.

I had always been on good terms with him.

An extra buck or two for finding me a parking space on Christopher Street. A quiet chat late at night when he was on duty. A cup of coffee when he couldn't sneak away for one. So why had he jammed it in when my back was turned? He had done it for a couple of bucks, stringer's fee.

Because Jerry, gentle reader, was one of the Common Man-types everyone lauds. He was and is a sample of the great ethic and morality of the Common Man in our time.

Jerry had done what he could do for two bucks, and within 24 hours I found myself referred to as: "Oh, yeah, Ellison. Isn't he the writer that got picked up on the junk charge?"

And as I went upstairs to catch a shave and change out of my cruddy clothes, clothes I'd slept in the night before, on a hardwood slab . . . as I went upstairs to shave my face and alter my thinking about the world in general . . . as I prepared my thinking for courts and lawyers and trials and possibly (now that I'd sampled the System) a jail sentence, I considered Jerry as a symbol:

What good is it? You try to make it in the game, you ply your trade the best way you can, and you don't step on any more necks than are absolutely necessary to keep you in the running, you begin to think you're doing okay and you have friends and you're not too bad a guy, and what good does it do?

The Common Man is on the scene. He'll play with another man's life and career for revenge—Ken Bales, are you there? I haven't forgotten—or for a lark, or out of misguided idiocy, or for a couple of dollars . . . and you've had it. There are guys who will wash someone down the drain to get two or five or fifty bucks from the *Daily News* for a not-quite-accurate tip. There are newspapermen who will go for news even if it isn't really news: *To hell with him; if we're wrong we'll run a retraction.*

Yeah, sure.

Accuse him in twelve-point type on the front page and five days later say he's innocent in an eight-point box on page thirty-six. Who remembers the retractions?

Who do you curse? That's the question. God help us all. That's the big thing: who do you blame? Do you blame the Authorities who are too busy keeping their ever-loving System running to be concerned about humanity? Do you blame the times, and its stamp of financial necessity? Who do you slug in the mouth? Who do you fight when you can't fight City Hall?

On October 31st, 1961, before a duly authorized Grand Jury panel, I was "severally discharged from their Undertaking to Answer" on the charges for which I'd been arraigned on September 12th. They passed down "no true bill" which meant I was an innocent man. But though I received my Certificate of Dismissal of Complaint (a copy of which occupies the next page), the repercussions of my arrest are still to be considered.

Friends from all over the country wrote asking if I needed either (1) financial aid, (2) the name of a good lawyer, (3) character witnesses, (4) pall-bearers or (5) a cure for narcotics addiction.

Lawsuits were instigated, then killed, to garner damages from the wire services and individual newspapers who had run the piece on my arrest. What was the use in taking something to court when we couldn't win ... their language was lovely. Yellow and obscure and all by inference.

My prints and mug shots are still on file in the New York Police Department.

I have a record, of sorts.

But all that is very minor indeed. All that is petty next to the good that came out of my last trip through Hell. I found who my real friends were ... a bearded jazz critic who very often had to take back empty Pepsi bottles to get food for the table, who was willing to fork over every cent he had to bail me out ... a girl who spent most of her time partying and wondering who she really was, who had no difficulty recognizing her place when a buddy needed help ... all the people I'd known, who wrote me asking if they could help in some way ... the editors who called and said they might find me story-assignments if I had to make lawyers' fees ... *The Village Voice*, its editor, Daniel Wolf, and its publisher, Ed Fancher, who asked me to write my story for their pages, in one of the finest liberal newspapers in the country ... the publishers of Regency Books, who read that little Greenwich Village newspaper piece, and commissioned me to write this book ...

And the display of sincerity, honest judgment and decency shown me by Mrs. Marion Walsh of the District Attorney's Office of the City of New York, and the honor-

COURT OF GENERAL SESSIONS
OF THE
COUNTY OF NEW YORK

Clerk's Office, —————— November 14, ——— 19 60

THE PEOPLE OF THE STATE OF
NEW YORK

against

HARLAN ELLISON

ON COMPLAINT FOR
1897 P.L.

No. 3926 - 60

Dated,   September 12,   19 60

I DO CERTIFY that it appears from an examination of the Record of Complaints on file in this office that the above complaint was dismissed by the Grand Jury, on   October 31,   , 19 60 , at the   October   Term, 19 60 and the said   Harlan Ellison

and his surety

were severally discharged from their Undertaking to Answer.

F. Howard Barrett

F. HOWARD BARRETT
Clerk of Court.

203

able ladies and gentlemen of the Grand Jury panel that sat in judgment of my case. The hard work and direct approach of my lawyer, Herb Plever, who knew there was no sense in wasting time with hanky-panky and fancy Perry Mason tactics when a simple laying-out of the facts would prove my innocence.

These were things that have partially offset my feelings of sorrow and bitterness and hatred at the things I saw in the Tombs, and seven years before, in the streets of Brooklyn.

Partially, because I wonder who will cry for the old men, and for the young men, in a society that has spent so much time making everyone equal that now "we are all so equal, we're nothing." Jerry the Doorman, do you hear?

Or as John Mason Brown has said:

Is the Common Man too common?

I've got this Common-Man Wind-Up Doll, see. You just wind it up, set it down on a table . . .

. . . and it finks on you.

HARLAN'S COLLECTION
JOIN NOW!

Hitler Painted Roses. I Have No Mouth & I Must Scream. Jeffty Is Five. The Deathbird. "Repent, Harlequin!" Said The Ticktockman. A Boy And His Dog. Shatterday. The Beast That Shouted Love At The Heart Of The World. Paingod. The Prowler In The City At The Edge Of The World. Shattered Like A Glass Goblin. Grail. Strange Wine.

They were all written by the same man. But you have never fully experienced these singular stories until you've heard them read by their creator. His personal appearances are few and far between. But now…Announcing

THE HARLAN ELLISON
RECORD COLLECTION

You are invited to become a charter member of the most innovative record society for the spoken word ever devised. An initial five dollar fee will bring you a quarterly newsletter of The Collection and the privilege of obtaining new, never-before-released, top-quality record albums of Harlan Ellison reading his award-winning stories.

Rabbit Hole, the newsletter, contains regular contributions from the author — segments of works-in-progress, inside information about the BUG JACK BARRON film (for Universal Pictures, to be directed by Costa-Gavras), and HE's other cinematic work, schedules of his lectures, photos and ...

The $5.00 annual fee covers the cost of the quarterly Newsletter and membership in The Collection. (The membership fee is $10.00 outside Canada and the United States.) For **members of The Collection only,** the records are available for $7.95 each plus $1.00 for postage and handling. ($4.00 for postage and handling for one or more foreign orders; $2.00 for Canadian orders.)

Our first new selection is Harlan reading JEFFTY IS FIVE, the fabulous story that won the Hugo, Nebula, Jupiter and British Fantasy awards; plus a brand new, meant-to-be-heard story, "Prince Myshkin, and Pass the Relish."

Our second new release is ON THE ROAD WITH ELLISON, a compendium of live, in-person excerpts from Harlan's recent appearances on radio, television, and in concert lectures at universities across The Great American Heartland.

To join The Collection, please send $5.00
for 4 issues of RABBIT HOLE
in check or money order to:

The Harlan Ellison Record Collection
420 South Beverly Drive, Suite 207
Beverly Hills, California 90212

Please add $8.95 for each record ordered.

(This offer valid through December 31, 1985.)